DEATH of a WITCH

The Hamish Macbeth series

Death of a Gossip
Death of a Cad
Death of an Outsider
Death of a Perfect Wife
Death of a Hussy
Death of a Snob
Death of a Prankster
Death of a Glutton
Death of a Travelling Man
Death of a Charming Man
Death of a Nag
Death of a Macho Man
Death of a Dentist
Death of a Scriptwriter
A Highland Christmas
Death of an Addict
Death of a Dustman
Death of a Celebrity
Death of a Village
Death of a Poison Pen
Death of a Bore
Death of a Dreamer
Death of a Maid
Death of a Gentle Lady
Death of a Witch
Death of a Valentine

DEATH of a WITCH

A Hamish Macbeth Murder Mystery

M. C. BEATON

ROBINSON
London

Constable & Robinson Ltd
3 The Lanchesters
162 Fulham Palace Road
London W6 9ER
www.constablerobinson.com

First published in the USA 2009 by
Grand Central Publishing, Hachette Book Group USA,
237 Park Avenue, New York, NY 10017

First UK edition published by Constable,
an imprint of Constable & Robinson Ltd 2009

This paperback edition published by Robinson,
an imprint of Constable & Robinson Ltd 2010

A copy of the British Library Cataloguing in Publication data is available from the British Library

ISBN: 978-1-84529-964-4 (pbk)
ISBN: 978-1-84529-918-7 (hbk)

Printed and bound in the EU

1 3 5 7 9 10 8 6 4 2

For Rene and Carole of Stow-on-the-Wold,
with affection

Hamish Macbeth fans share their reviews . . .

'Treat yourself to an adventure in the Highlands; remember your coffee and scones – for you'll want to stay a while!'

'I do believe I am in love with Hamish.'

'M. C. Beaton's stories are absolutely excellent . . . Hamish is a pure delight!'

'A highly entertaining read that will have me hunting out the others in the series.'

'A new Hamish Macbeth novel is always a treat.'

'Once I read the first mystery I was hooked . . . I love her characters.'

Share your own reviews and comments at www.constablerobinson.com

Chapter One

By the pricking of my thumbs,
Something wicked this way comes.
– William Shakespeare

Police Constable Hamish Macbeth, heading home to his police station in the village of Lochdubh in Sutherland, heaved a sigh of relief. He stopped for a moment by the side of the road and rolled down the car window. He was driving a battered old Rover, manufactured before the days of power steering and electronic windows.

Hamish breathed in all the familiar scents of the Scottish Highlands: peat smoke, wild thyme, pine and salt air blown in on the Atlantic gales from the coast.

Urged by his friend Angela Brodie to go abroad on holiday for once in his life, Hamish had opted for a cheap off-season package trip to the south of Spain.

His hopes of a holiday romance had been dashed as soon as he arrived. The hotel, ambitiously named The Royal Britannia, catered for British old-age pensioners who wanted to escape the winter back home and the heating bills that came with it. He was in great demand at tea dances, as the other guests were mostly sprightly ladies in their sixties and seventies. When he tried to escape from the hotel food, which was designed for the British palate – chips with everything – and went to some little Spanish restaurant, he would find that several of the ladies had followed him only to become amorous over jugs of sangria. Cursed with innate highland courtesy, he could not find it in him to be rude enough to get rid of them.

But now he was heading home. He had bought the old banger of a car to leave at Inverness airport when he started his journey, not wanting to use the police Land Rover and so incur the wrath of his bosses.

Hamish started off again as the car coughed and spluttered, threatening to collapse at each steep hill like a weary horse.

At last he drove over the hump backed bridge and into the village of Lochdubh.

He uncoiled his long length from the little car and stood up and stretched. Fingers of rain were blowing down the sea loch, but there was a patch of blue over to the west heralding better weather to come. Although it was November, the proximity of the Gulf Stream meant there were often mild days.

Then for some reason he could not explain, he began to feel uneasy. It seemed that the very air was full of some vague threat.

He shook himself impatiently, unlocked the police station door, and went in.

There was a note from Angela lying on the kitchen table. It read: 'Hamish, this is the very last time I look after your pets for you. Come and collect them as soon as you can, Angela.'

Hamish owned a mongrel called Lugs and a domesticated wild cat called Sonsie. Angela Brodie was the doctor's wife. He went out again and walked to Angela's cottage. The cat and dog looked at him sullenly as if he was not to be forgiven for having left them.

'About time, too,' said Angela crossly.

'They weren't too much trouble, surely?' said Hamish.

'They kept escaping and going to look for you and I had the gamekeeper, Willie, and several of the others up on the braes to hunt them down and bring them back. Oh, well, sit down and have a coffee and tell me about your trip. Lots of sunshine, pretty girls?'

'I'm glad to be home, and I don't want to talk about it,' said Hamish.

The wild cat put a large paw on Hamish's leg and gave a low hiss. Lugs, a shaggy dog with floppy ears and odd blue eyes, stared up at Hamish accusingly.

Hamish sat down at the cluttered kitchen table where Angela's cats roamed among the unwashed breakfast dishes. Looking at Angela, with her wispy hair and gentle face, Hamish wondered, not for the first time, how a doctor's wife could be so unhygienic.

'I had an offer for your cat while you were away,' said Angela, putting a mug of coffee down in front of him. 'Most insistent, she was. Last offer was a hundred pounds.'

'Who are you talking about?'

'Of course, you don't know. We've got a newcomer. She bought Sandy Ross's cottage.'

'Must have got it for a song,' said Hamish. 'That place has only a corrugated iron roof and an outside toilet. Who is she?'

'Catriona Beldame.'

'What sort of a name is that? Is she foreign?'

'No, she has a bit of a highland accent.'

'And where's she from?'

'Nobody knows. She just arrived. She's . . . well, odd.'

'How odd?'

'She gives me the shivers. She's very tall, as tall as you, and she has a queer sort of medieval face, very white, and yellowish brown eyes with heavy white lids. She has a long thin nose and a small mouth. She saw your cat and decided she must have it. There's something else.'

'What else?'

'Some of the local men have been seen visiting her late at night.'

'Dinnae tell me Lochdubh's got its own brothel at last!'

'That's not it. I think she supplies herbal medicines.'

'So why men, why late at night? Why no women?'

'That's the odd thing. No one talks about it. The Currie sisters said something to me about the men visiting her and then they clammed up.'

'Not like that precious pair,' commented Hamish. The Currie sisters were spinster twins and usually a great fund of gossip, some of it at Hamish's expense. 'I'd better go and visit this newcomer.'

'If you can find the time. Detective Chief Inspector Blair has been demanding to know when you're getting back. He said that you're to report to police headquarters in Strathbane as soon as you arrive.'

'Why?'

'It might be because some gang has been robbing all the little local post offices in the north. Lochinver was attacked last week and then Altnabuie. You know how it is. They think we're easy pickings this far north and with only one policeman to cover hundreds and hundreds of square miles.'

Hamish returned to the station, changed into his uniform, helped his pets into the police Land Rover, and set off over the hills.

As he drove down the long slope that led to Strathbane, he thought the town really was a blot on the beauty of the highland landscape with its decaying docks, crumbling tower blocks, vice and crime.

Steady rain was beginning to fall as he walked up the steps of headquarters and made his way up to the detectives' room.

Detective Sergeant Jimmy Anderson cried, 'Well, if it isn't *señor* back from Spain! Bring me a present?'

'Some duty-free whisky.'

'Got it with you?'

'Back at the station.'

Hamish noticed that Jimmy's usually sharp foxy face was getting blurred round the edges and his blue eyes were watery. The amount the detective drank was at last beginning to show.

'What's all this about burglaries?' asked Hamish.

'Lot of them at wee post offices.'

'What's been done about it?'

'Nothing much. The territory's huge and we

never know where they'll hit next. Blair wants to see you.'

The man himself lumbered out of his office. He was a thickset Glaswegian who loathed Hamish.

'There you are, you teuchter,' he snarled. 'Anderson, gie him what we've got on thae burglaries. I want a quick result.'

Blair went back into his office and slammed the door.

'I've printed off all the reports for you,' said Jimmy. 'It's always the same. Three men, masked wi' balaclavas. One wi' a sawn-off shotgun. Nobody's been hurt so far.'

'Any undercover cops been sent out to hide in the post offices?' asked Hamish.

'Aye, for a bit. But the villains always chose the one there wasn't a cop in.'

Hamish pulled out a chair and sat down. 'Now, there's a thing. Could it be possible that some cheil here was giving them information?'

'Aw, come on, Hamish. It's hardly the Great Train Robbery we're talking about.'

'Who's the newest policeman on the force?'

'Policewoman. Wee Alice Donaldson.'

'Where is she right now?'

'Off duty today. Och, Hamish. You just can't think . . .'

'Of anything else,' said Hamish. 'Let me have her address.'

Jimmy applied himself to the computer and

then said, 'Here it is. Write it down. Eight Bannoch Brae. That's down near the docks. Not a tower block. There's a row of wee houses just before you get to the tower blocks on the Inverness Road.'

'And what's she like?'

'Neat, quiet. Come on, laddie. You've had too much sun.'

'It iss worth a try,' said Hamish angrily, the sudden sibilance of his accent showing he was uneasy. 'I haff nothing else to go on.'

'Suit yourself. Did you get laid?'

But Hamish was already walking away.

When Hamish left headquarters, the wind had risen. Rain slashed into his face as he hurried to the Land Rover.

He found Bannoch Brae and parked outside number 8. 'Won't be long,' he said to his animals. 'Sit there and shut up and I'll buy ye a fish supper on the road home.'

There was a weedy garden in front of a small stone house. Hamish went up to the front door and rang the bell.

The door opened and a girl stood looking up at him. She was not very tall. Two wings of black hair hung on either side of a thin face.

'Alice Donaldson?' asked Hamish.

'Yes, that's me. It's my day off. Am I wanted back on duty?'

'No, I chust wanted to be having a wee word with you.'

'Come in.'

She stood aside to let him past and then closed the door and ushered him into a small front room.

The room seemed rather bleak. It was simply furnished with a three-piece suite and a paraffin heater in front of the empty fireplace.

'Sit down,' said Alice. 'Tea?'

'No, thank you. I'm chust back from Spain and I haff been asked to investigate the burglaries of the post offices,' said Hamish, nervously wondering why his imagination had leapt to the conclusion that some member of the force had been tipping off the gang.

'Oh, yes? How can I help? I haven't had anything to do with any of the cases.'

Hamish could not see much of her face because of those wings of hair. Didn't they irritate her?

She was wearing a man's shirt tied at the waist and a pair of worn jeans. His hazel eyes suddenly sharpened.

'What are you staring at?' she demanded.

'That looks like a cigarette burn on your neck,' said Hamish.

Her hand fluttered up to the burn. 'It's nothing. I'm clumsy.'

Hamish looked around the room. He could not see any ashtray; neither could he smell smoke. If she smoked, he thought, then the fabric upholstery would have retained some of the smell.

He was sitting at one end of the sofa and Alice was in an armchair next to him.

Hamish leaned forward suddenly and swept a wing of her hair back from her face. There was a black-and-yellow bruise on her cheek. She jerked her head back, and the other wing of hair flew back. The other side of her face was bruised as well.

'Who did this to ye, lassie?' asked Hamish gently.

'No one!' Her voice was shrill. 'I'm clumsy. This is my day off. You've no right . . .'

'They beat you up for information, didn't they?' said Hamish. 'Do you know them, or did they just pick on you?'

She began to cry. Great sobs racked her body. Hamish waited patiently. He felt that if he comforted her, she might take it as a sign of weakness.

He took a handkerchief out of his pocket and handed it to her. It had been given to him by one of his admirers at the Spanish hotel who had even embroidered his initials in one corner.

At last she wiped her eyes and looked at him bleakly. 'I'm finished with the force.'

'Let's hear it,' said Hamish.

In a flat tired voice she told him what had happened. She had been out clubbing in

Strathbane and had got picked up by a man, George MacDuff. They had gone out for a bit and then one evening he had come round with two friends, Hugh Sutherland and Andy Burnside. George had said the police were staking out post offices and they wanted her to tell them which ones. She refused. George got nasty. They tied her to a chair and stripped off her blouse and began to burn her with cigarettes. She said she was terrified and told them she would find out for them.

'You had their names and descriptions,' said Hamish. 'Why didn't you just report them?'

'George knows where my mother lives in Bonar Bridge. He said if I told anyone, they would kill her.'

'Lassie, the police could have put your mother under protection.'

'With Blair in charge?'

'Oh, well, maybe you have a point. What's the next job?'

'They came round today. I said I wouldn't tell them anything more and they beat me. I still wouldn't tell them but they hurt me so much, I told them that the post offices were no longer under surveillance. George said something like "Leave her." Then as they went out, I heard one of the others say, "Braikie tomorrow'll be our last anyway." I'd better get my coat. You'll be taking me in.'

'Let me think.' Hamish ran his long fingers

through his flaming red hair. 'Who's your doctor?'

'Dr Sing.'

'Sympathetic?'

'He seemed like a nice man. I only saw him the once when I had a sprained ankle.'

'Get me his number.'

Supplied with the phone number, Hamish phoned Dr Sing and asked him to call, adding that it was a police matter.

'What are you going to do?' asked Alice.

'Try to get you out of this.'

When Dr Sing arrived, Hamish said, 'Miss Donaldson has been beaten up during some undercover work. We fear this might be because of some informant at headquarters. Until we investigate further, we want you to sign her off for two weeks suffering from injuries incurred after a bad fall down the stairs. You would be helping an investigation considerably if you could do this.'

Dr Sing was a young doctor, recently qualified and anxious to please. He wrote out the certificate and would have examined Alice but Hamish said a police doctor had already had a look. 'But the certificate has to be issued by her own doctor,' said Hamish.

When the doctor had left, Hamish said, 'Get over to your mother in Bonar Bridge and get her off to a wee hotel somewhere until this blows over. Now, if these men are caught and your name comes up, don't say I had anything to do with it or we'll both be out of the force.'

'I don't know how to thank you,' said Alice.

'Just move fast and get out of here,' said Hamish. 'Have you got a car?' She nodded. 'Pack quickly and off you go!'

Hamish stopped on the road back to Lochdubh and bought three fish suppers to feed his pets and himself, wondering all the time how to catch the men who proposed robbing the Braikie Post Office. They were getting bolder, he thought. The others had mainly been sub post offices in general stores, but Braikie was a pedigree one and quite new. No one could understand how Braikie, a remote highland town, should get a new post office when the government was proposing to close so many down.

Twice Hamish had been promoted to sergeant and twice he had been demoted. During the two periods he had held the rank of sergeant, he had policemen working under him. One was Willie Lamont, who had married the daughter of an Italian restaurant owner and left to work in the restaurant. The other, Clarry Graham, was now employed as a chef at the Tommel Castle Hotel. He decided to get them to help him. If he got a squad from Strathbane, they would insist on knowing how he got the information about the proposed robbery. Or Blair might take over and make a mess of it.

Hamish had a sudden image of Blair being blasted to death by a shotgun and he smiled. It was great that some of the things inside his head never got to the outside, he thought.

In the morning, Hamish, flanked by Clarry and Willie, broke the news to the alarmed postmistress, Ellie Macpherson, that he expected the place to be raided. Unfortunately for Hamish, Ellie was the leading light of the local dramatic society and also a sort of female Walter Mitty. He had managed to talk to her just before she opened up in the morning. Ellie, a scrawny woman who jangled with cheap jewellery, drew herself up and said, 'I shall throw myself on the guns!' Her eyes were half-closed. Hamish repressed a sigh. He guessed Ellie was already seeing herself on the front page of some newspaper.

'You'll do nothing of the sort,' snapped Hamish. 'You'll lie down behind your counter as soon as they come in. Now, Willie and Clarry here will be in the post office, looking at cards or something. They've got their shotguns and if anyone asks, they'll say they are going out hunting rabbits up on the braes.'

The day dragged on. Hamish, hidden in the back shop, yawned and fidgeted. Willie and

Clarry, tired of reading the rhymes of the greeting cards to each other, yawned as well with boredom.

Just when Hamish was beginning to fear that the robbers planned to attack somewhere else, the door of the post office was thrown open. He heard the customers scream and a man's voice say, 'Hand over the money or you'll get shot.'

Hamish darted out of the back of the shop, holding his own shotgun. He trod on the prone figure of Ellie, who screamed.

Willie was holding his shotgun against the neck of the one armed man who had dropped his gun to the floor, and Clarry was covering the other two. Hamish leapt over the counter and, taking out three sets of handcuffs, arrested and cautioned the robbers.

Blair was furious when he got the news. 'Whit was that loon daein' playing the lone sheriff?' he said to Chief Superintendent Peter Daviot.

'Now, now,' said Daviot. 'Hamish has got these men and I am not going to quibble about the way he did it.'

Jimmy Anderson waylaid Hamish as he was on his way out of headquarters after typing up a full report.

'So was Alice the informant?' he asked.

'No, nothing to do with it. Chust a lucky guess on my part.'

'She's not in today.'

'Och, the lassie had a bad fall. I called her doctor and he told her to take a couple of weeks off.'

'Aye, right,' said Jimmy cynically.

'Come over to Lochdubh one evening,' said Hamish. 'Don't forget, I've a bottle for you.'

Hamish was just sitting down wearily to an evening meal of Scotch pie and peas when someone knocked at the door.

'Come in,' he shouted. 'The door's open.'

Alice walked in. 'I heard about it on the evening news,' she said. 'Did they say anything about me?'

'No, I'd have heard. They're not going to confess to beating someone up for information. They'll all be sent away for a long time. You can get drunk and run someone over in your car and get a suspended sentence, but if you steal money then the full weight of the courts comes down on your head. Sit down. I hope you've eaten, because this is all I've got.'

'Yes, I did have something earlier. So I can move back home?'

'Certainly. None of that lot will be getting out on bail.'

She sat down with a sigh. 'I'm going to hand in my resignation.'

'Why?'

'I'm just not cut out for the force. It's not really because of the beating. I don't have much courage. I'm going back to university to get a degree and then maybe I'll teach.'

'If that's what you want to do . . .'

'But we can see each other sometimes?'

'Maybe. I do haff the girlfriend, you know.'

'Oh, well, I'd better be on my way.'

Hamish saw her out, finished his meal, undressed, showered and went to bed, stretching out with a groan of relief. There were two thumps and the cat and dog got into bed with him.

A gale was howling outside, wailing round the building like a banshee. Before he plunged into sleep, Hamish found he was experiencing a stab of superstitious dread. Must be that pie, was his last waking thought.

The morning was glittering with yellow sunlight. Wisps of high cloud raced across a washed-out blue sky, and the waters of the loch were churned up into angry choppy waves.

Hamish put on his uniform of serge trousers, blue shirt, dark blue tie and police sweater with epaulettes. He put his peaked cap on his red hair. He noticed that his trousers were baggy at the knees.

He unlocked the large cat flap, big enough to let the dog in and out as well, and said to his pets, 'You stay here. I've got a visit to make.'

The wind sang in the heather as he made his way on foot to Sandy Ross's old cottage. Who was this Catriona Beldame that even the Currie sisters wouldn't gossip about?

He sensed someone behind him and swung round. The seer, Angus Macdonald, his long grey beard blowing in the wind, was shouting something, but his words were whipped away with the gale.

Hamish waited until Angus caught up with him. 'Dinnae go there, Hamish,' panted the seer.

'Why not,' said Hamish, rocking slightly in the force of the wind and holding on to his peaked cap.

'Because she's a witch, that's why,' said Angus. 'She's brought evil to Lochdubh.'

'Havers,' said Hamish. 'What's she doing? Setting up in competition?'

'I'm warning ye, Hamish. Black days are coming. I see blood.'

'Och, away wi' ye,' said Hamish. 'There's no such thing as witches.'

'On your ain head be it,' said Angus and turned away.

Hamish walked on, hoping that old Angus

wasn't beginning to suffer from the onset of Alzheimer's.

The cottage had no garden. The springy heather went right up to the door. It was a low one-storey whitewashed building with a red corrugated iron roof.

As he approached the door, a large black cloud swept across the sun and all at once the wind died.

Again Hamish felt that odd stab of superstitious dread. Then the wind started up again and the cloud moved from the sun.

Hamish raised his hand to the weather-beaten knocker on the door.

Chapter Two

La Belle Dame sans Merci
Hath thee in thrall!
– John Keats

The woman who answered the door fitted the description Angela had given him. And yet, as she stood there, looking at him inquiringly, Hamish decided there was nothing sinister about her. She had a dab of flour on one cheek and she was wearing an old Aran sweater, dusty blue corduroy trousers, and sneakers.

'I am the local constable,' said Hamish. 'I have been away on holiday and have only just heard of your arrival.'

'Come in,' she said.

The kitchen-cum-living room into which she led him was stone-flagged. A peat fire smouldered on the hearth. Bookshelves lined one wall and on another, on either side of the low door, shelves held a variety of glass bottles. In the centre of the room was a scarred oak table surrounded by six high-backed Orkney chairs.

The kitchen part consisted of a sink and butane gas cooker, a granite top with pine cupboards above and below. There was neither a fridge nor a washing machine.

'Please sit down,' she said. Her voice was low and mellow with only a slight trace of highland accent.

Hamish sat down at the table and removed his cap. Despite the fire, the room was cold and the wind soughed through the heather outside the house with an urgent whispering sound.

'What brought you to this part?' asked Hamish.

'It's a pretty village,' she said. 'Would you like some tea?'

'I'd prefer coffee.'

'I only have herbal tea. Good for you.'

'All right,' said Hamish. 'Although I find that things that are said to be good for me are not very appealing.'

She smiled an enchanting smile that lit up her face. 'Oh, you'll like this.'

'Where did you come from?' asked Hamish as she busied herself at the counter by putting a kettle on the cooker.

'Oh, here and there.'

'And where was the last there?'

'Dear me. You do go on like a policeman. So many questions!'

'What do you do for a living?' pursued Hamish.

'I supply therapy and herbal treatments.'

'Have many of the villagers visited you? I believe quite a few men have called on you.'

'I have a good treatment for sexual dysfunction. Want some?'

'I do not haff the trouble in that department,' said Hamish, blushing. 'What exactly is this treatment?'

'A secret recipe.'

Hamish said stiffly, 'We do not go in for sex much in Lochdubh,' and immediately felt silly as she turned round and looked at him with amusement.

She put a cup of tea in front of him and said, 'Now, try that.'

Hamish took a cautious sip. It was some sort of fruit tea, he guessed, very pleasant to the taste.

Catriona sat down at the table close to him and raised her own cup to her lips. She looked at him over the rim and smiled.

'Tell me about your sex life.'

'Chust keep your nose out o' my private life,' said Hamish sharply.

'But you've been asking me so many personal questions. Isn't it fair I should ask you some?'

'I didnae ask you about your sex life.'

Her knee pressed against his under the table.

'I don't mind. For example, I'm very good in bed.'

'Are you running a brothel here?' demanded Hamish.

She threw back her head and laughed. Then she said, 'My dear man, if I wanted to run a brothel, I would hardly settle in a village in the north of Scotland. Let's not quarrel.' She covered his hand with her own. 'I simply supply a few herbal medicines. I was teasing you. The main complaint here is indigestion.'

He felt a sudden tug of attraction. He drew his hand away gently.

'I must be off,' he said, standing up and putting on his cap. 'I only called to introduce myself.'

'Call again,' said Catriona.

She turned in the doorway and kissed him on the cheek. 'See you very soon,' she said.

Hamish walked off down the brae. He felt strangely elated. All of a sudden, he wanted to turn back and ask her out for dinner.

He half-turned back. She was still standing in the doorway, watching him. Hamish forced himself to keep on going.

The desire to go back and see her lasted until he ate a substantial lunch and then he scratched his head in bewilderment. What had come over him? Had there been something in that tea?

He got a call from Jimmy Anderson reminding him that he was expected in the sheriff's court in Strathbane at three o'clock that afternoon, along with Willie Lamont and Clarry Graham. Hamish phoned both Willie and Clarry and suggested they should all go together.

Willie was seated next to Hamish in the front passenger seat and Clarry was in the back. At one point in the drive, Hamish said, 'Willie, are you scratching yourself?'

Willie removed his hand from his crotch. 'I think I've got a wee bit o' cystitis.'

'Then see Dr Brodie as soon as possible. Man, what if ye were to go on like that in court?'

The proceedings did not take long. In vain did the defence advocate plead that his clients were truly remorseful. The sheriff said the case was too severe to be tried in his court; he was remanding the burglars without bail to appear at the high court in Edinburgh.

'I'll drop you off at Dr Brodie's,' said Hamish.

'I've got to get to the restaurant,' said Willie. 'I'll maybe drop along later.'

'Don't leave it too long. Cystitis can be nasty,' said Hamish.

* * *

Hamish found a message from Dr Brodie when he got to the police station, asking him to call urgently.

He said to Sonsie and Lugs, 'No, you pair stay here. I think Angela's had enough of ye.'

As he walked along the waterfront, he felt the village was strangely quiet. Again he was assailed by a feeling of foreboding.

Dr Brodie led Hamish into his cluttered living room. Cold ash spilled out over the grate.

'What's the problem?' asked Hamish.

'Several of my male patients have been coming to me with swollen genitalia and inflammation of the urinary tract.'

'So?'

'I treated a case like this when I was much younger and an army doctor. It turned out to be Spanish fly.'

'I've read about that somewhere. Isn't it an aphrodisiac?'

'It's supposed to be. It's from a beetle that is crushed into powder. It creates the illusion of increased sexual activity but all it does is harm, and it can damage the kidneys badly.'

'I've heard a lot of the men have been visiting Catriona Beldame,' said Hamish. 'Do you think she's been supplying the stuff?'

'I tried to get them to admit it but not one of them would. I believe they think she's a witch thanks to Angus shooting his mouth off. People here are still very superstitious.'

'I'll get up to her place right away,' said Hamish. 'Either she lets me examine what she's got in those bottles or I'll get a search warrant.'

Hamish hurried to the police station to get some material and put in a request for a search warrant, deciding it would be a good idea to get one in case she proved difficult. Then he went along the waterfront, stopping abruptly at the sight of Archie Maclean hurling a small glass bottle into the loch.

'What are you doing?' asked Hamish, hurrying up to him.

'Naethin'. Chust some medicine that didnae work.'

'You got it from the Beldame woman. You, Archie? Wanting to improve your sexual prowess?'

Archie hung his head. 'It seemed like the good idea, but, och, herself wasnae having any of it. "Leave me alone," she says, "or I'll throw ye in the loch." I went tae the doctor and he telt me to get rid of it.'

'I wish you'd kept it,' said Hamish. 'I'm off up there now to put a stop to her. God, I could kill that woman.'

After Hamish strode off, Archie went into the bar on the waterfront and bought himself a pint of Export. 'She's getting her comeuppance,' he said to the men gathered at the bar. 'Our Hamish says he's going tae kill her.'

Once again Catriona opened the door to Hamish and invited him in. 'This is not a social call,' said Hamish, taking out a number of glassine envelopes. 'Either you let me examine what you have in those jars or I'll get a search warrant.'

'My dear man, go right ahead. I have nothing to hide.'

Her eyes widened as Hamish took out packets of glassine envelopes and a small spoon. 'I'll just collect a bit of each,' he said, moving towards the shelves.

She darted in front of him.

'Get the search warrant,' she hissed, 'and a curse on you.'

'So you do have something to hide.'

'I've nothing to hide,' she panted. 'I don't like you ferreting around and poking your nose into my affairs. Get out!'

On his return to the police station, Hamish got a message to phone Blair. Reluctantly, he called police headquarters and was put through to Blair.

'Whit's this about a search warrant?' chuckled Blair.

'It's important,' said Hamish.

'Important, what?'

'Important, *sir*. The damn woman is poisoning the village.'

'You're all sae backwards up there, it's a wonder ye ken the difference.'

'I wanted to examine her potions,' said Hamish patiently, 'and she refused to let me take samples.'

'Anyone died?'

'No, but . . .'

'Listen, laddie, we've got real crimes here – gangs and drugs and mayhem. Until you've got yourself a real crime, forget it.'

'What do I have to do?' raged Hamish. 'Kill her?'

Blair slammed down the phone.

Hamish sat until his rage had died down. He decided to make himself some comfort food for dinner. He boiled a small haggis and served it with mashed turnip and mashed potatoes. His pets had already been fed and were fast asleep.

He allowed himself one small glass of whisky while he wondered what he could do about the witch.

I'll threaten her, he decided. I'll go up there right now and tell her I'll make her life one hell on earth unless she either leaves or quits selling quack medicine.

The wind had dropped. There was a clear starry sky and frost glittering on the ground as he set off.

But although there was a light shining through her cottage window, there was no reply to his knock.

Ina Braid was sixty-three. She was married to Fergus, who worked at a paper mill over in Strathbane.

Theirs had always appeared to be a comfortable marriage. Tucked up beside her husband in their double bed that evening, Ina opened a romance called *Highland Heart*, removed the bookmark, and settled against the pillows to read. She had just got to the exciting bit where the laird grabbed the village girl in his strong arms and bent his head to hers.

'What about a wee bit o' a cuddle,' said Fergus, trying to put his arms round her.

'Get off!' snapped Ina. 'What's come over ye?'

'We havenae done – you know – in a long while.'

'Because neither of us has wanted to. Leave me alone!'

'I want ma marital rights. Come here!'

Ina leapt out of bed and stood there, panting. 'Keep away from me or I'll stab ye wi' the bread knife.'

'Ye frigid wee hoor!' roared Fergus.

Something very like that confrontation went on behind several closed doors in the village of Lochdubh.

Hamish was approaching his station from a field at the back where he had been giving his small flock of sheep their winter feed when he found the minister's wife waiting for him.

Mrs Wellington was the epitome of Highland respectability from her waxed coat and brogues to the felt hat with the pheasant's feather in it on her head.

'Come ben,' said Hamish. 'Trouble?'

'Bad trouble,' said Mrs Wellington.

'Coffee?'

'Strong, black and with a dram in it.'

'Bad night?'

'Up most of the night with calls from distressed women.'

'Wait till I get your coffee and you can tell me all about it.' Hamish put on the kettle and took a half-bottle of whisky down from a shelf.

When he had served Mrs Wellington, he asked, 'Now, what is going on?'

Mrs Wellington took a fortifying pull of her brew and said, 'Sex.'

'Sex?'

'I am being asked for help by some women in the village whose husbands have started pestering them just when they thought all that nonsense was over. Just imagine it, Hamish. A woman settling down for the night as she has done for years with a good book and being subjected to . . . that.'

Poor old minister, thought Hamish.

'I think I know what's at the back of it,' said Hamish, 'and yes, I can put a stop to it. Tomorrow is the Sabbath. Tell your man I want to borrow his pulpit to make an announcement.'

'What about?'

'I'd rather break the news all at once.'

After the opening hymn was sung on Sunday, the villagers looked in surprise as Hamish climbed up to the pulpit.

'This may hardly seem a fit topic for a church,' said Hamish, 'but as it is causing misery in the village, I want to give all the men of Lochdubh a warning. If you have been going to a Miss Beldame for a potion to help your sexual prowess, it is the firm belief of Dr Brodie that what you have been taking is Spanish fly. This does not enhance your prowess. It swells the genitals and could cause damage to your kidneys. I will deal with Miss Beldame myself. None of you is to go near her.'

Shocked faces stared up at him. He surendered the pulpit to Mr Wellington and went and sat in a pew at the back.

At the end of the service, he slipped out of the church and went back to the police station. He planned to visit Catriona after he had eaten his lunch.

But there was a knock at the kitchen door and then the Currie sisters walked in.

'This is a bad business,' said Nessie.

'Bad business,' echoed Jessie, who always repeated the end of her sister's sentences.

'I thought you pair would ha' known about it before this,' said Hamish.

'We did,' said Nessie. 'But she's a witch!'

'A witch,' said Jessie.

'Look here. There are no such things as witches.'

'Keep your voice down,' hissed Nessie, looking furtively around.

'Voice down' came the Greek chorus.

Hamish sighed. He knew the highlanders were deeply superstitious.

'I'm going to deal with her,' he said firmly. 'By tomorrow, you'll have nothing to worry about. I'll kill her if I have to. Don't look like that. Just joking. Now, off with you.'

Hamish ate his lunch, fed his pets, told them to stay behind, and set off for Catriona Beldame's cottage. A group of villagers followed him. He kept turning and shouting 'Stay back!' and they would stop, but as soon as he moved on, they would follow again, keeping a discreet distance.

He knocked at the door. Catriona answered his knock and stood there, one hand on the lintel. She was dressed in a long black velvet gown that made her look like the witch she was supposed to be.

'Well?'

'I am here to tell you,' said Hamish, 'that if you continue to supply drugs to the people of this village, it will be the worse for you.'

She gave a mocking laugh. 'Couldn't get your search warrant, could you?'

He turned and looked at her Volvo, parked at the side of the cottage. He went over to it and shone his torch on it. 'You need new tyres,' he said. 'You cannot drive that car until you have them fitted. Your vehicle is not roadworthy.'

She followed him. The wind had risen and was whipping her hair about her face.

She pointed a long finger at him. 'I cursed you, remember?' she said. 'Black days are coming, Hamish Macbeth.'

'Oh, go to hell,' shouted Hamish. 'I'll haff ye out o' my village and on your broomstick if it's the last thing I do. Catriona Beldame, indeed. What's your real name, lassie? Tracy Smellie, Josie Clapp, something like that? I'll find out, you know.'

She flew at him, her hands clawing at his face.

He gave her a hearty push and she went sprawling in the heather.

Hamish went and stood over her. 'Take my advice and leave by tomorrow.'

He turned and strode away down the brae. The watchers had vanished.

The next day, a case of shoplifting took him over to Cnothan, his least favourite place. It turned out to be the theft of nothing more than chocolate bars. He identified the two culprits from the security camera, persuaded the angry shopkeeper not to press criminal charges, and went off to see the boys' parents. He was damned if he was going to give two little boys a criminal record this early in their lives. It all took more time than he had expected between getting the boys, two brothers, from school, and taking them home to their shocked mother. Mother and boys were then taken to the shop, where they apologized while the mother paid for the stolen goods. After that, he stopped off to see some friends in Cnothan before heading home.

He took his binoculars and went out on to the waterfront and focussed them on the 'witch's' cottage. Her car was still there. He wondered what to do. He was sure that if he arrested her, they would now not find anything sinister in those bottles of hers. She would have destroyed anything incriminating. If he threatened her any more, he could be charged with police harassment.

He returned to the station to find Jimmy Anderson waiting for him. 'You're going to be up on a disciplinary charge, Hamish, unless you can come up with a good explanation.'

'What are you talking about?'

'Your newcomer, Catriona Beldame, has reported you for assault.'

'She tried to claw my face, I pushed her over, and I've got witnesses. Come ben and get your whisky and I'll tell you all about it.'

Seated at the kitchen table a few minutes later, Jimmy listened to Hamish's story.

When Hamish had finished, he said, 'Why didn't the bampots just order Viagra from the Internet?'

'I don't think they'd know how to,' said Hamish. 'We're still a superstitious lot here. I checked the police files under her daft name, but I couldn't find anything. That woman is evil!'

'What is it with women?' asked Jimmy. 'You see all these magazines telling them how to enhance their sex life.'

'I think you'll find the complaining women all had children and were past the menopause. They'd rather read a romance or fantasize about a film star than have their old man fumbling again.'

'Miserable old biddies. They should let the old man get his leg over occasionally.'

'I hate it all,' said Hamish. 'I'm telling you, Jimmy, the two biggest motives for murder are sex and money.'

'Maybe she was supplying one and getting the other for services rendered,' suggested Jimmy.

'There's not that much money in Lochdubh.'

'Come on, man! I bet there's money hidden under some of the mattresses here. They're a canny lot. Probably have been saving for years.'

'I chust wish she would go away,' mourned Hamish. 'The men know she made a fool of them.'

The following two days were quiet. No sign of the witch, and yet Hamish swore he could almost see a miasma of evil hanging over his beloved village.

Then, on the third morning, he received a visit from the milkman, Hughie Cromart. 'The milk outside the Beldame woman's cottage hasn't been taken in,' he said. 'You should get up there and see if anything has happened to her.'

Hamish felt a spasm of black dread. The fear

that one of the men in the village would do something to the 'witch' that had been lurking around his subconscious now came roaring up into his brain.

'I'll get up there right away,' he said.

It was a crisp cold morning. There had been a thick frost during the night. The loch lay as still as a sheet of metal under a grey sky. The tops of the two mountains soaring above Lochdubh were covered in snow.

Two buzzards sailed lazily above the cottage as Hamish approached.

He knocked at the door and waited.

No reply.

He tried the handle but the door was locked. He then tried to peer into the two windows at the front of the cottage, but the curtains were drawn.

Hamish wondered what to do. If he broke in and she was all right, she would add the charge of breaking and entering to the one of police harassment. He walked round to the back.

There was one door and one window at the back, but the door was locked and the curtains were tightly drawn across the window.

He studied the lock. It was a simple Yale one. He took out a thin strip of metal and forced the lock.

Hamish switched on the light. He found himself in the room where she kept all her potions, the room he had been in before. He went across the tiny hall and opened the door to the room opposite.

It had been fitted up as a bedroom. He could see that in the dim light filtering through the curtains there was a figure on the bed. He switched on the light and let out a gasp of dismay.

Catriona was lying naked on the bed. Her throat had been slashed and there were stab wounds on her chest. Blood seemed to have spurted everywhere. He backed out slowly and made his way outside the way he came in.

Hamish phoned police headquarters and stood there, looking down the brae to the village, wondering who the murderer was and praying it wasn't one of the villagers.

Chapter Three

Wickedness is a myth invented by good people to account for the curious attraction of others.

– Oscar Wilde

Hamish stood outside the cottage waiting for the police from Strathbane to arrive. A group of villagers had gathered down the brae and stood looking at him in silence. It was unnerving. No one approached him or called out to him asking what was wrong.

As he heard the sirens in the distance, there was a sudden gasp from the crowd. He heard behind him a sinister crackling sound and swung round in alarm. The red glare of flames could be seen at the bedroom window where the dead body lay.

Hamish ran into the cottage. At least the body must be saved for the autopsy. But when he opened the bedroom door, he reeled back before a crackling wall of flame. He ran out again and round the back of the cottage. There was no sign of anyone. He called the fire brigade in Braikie and then ran down to the crowd, crying to them to fetch water. Deaf to his pleas, they turned as one person and began to walk away.

By the time the first police car arrived carrying Blair and Jimmy Anderson, the cottage was a roaring inferno.

'Whit the hell's going on here?' yelled Blair.

'It's Catriona Beldame,' said Hamish. 'Someone murdered her and then the cottage was set on fire.'

Hamish realized, in that moment, that the murderer had probably been lurking in the cottage and set fire to the place as soon as he had walked outside. What had happened to his usual highland sixth sense? He could have sworn he was alone in the place.

'So,' said Blair, 'how do ye know she was murdered?'

'There was a report from the milkman that she hadn't been taking in her milk. I went in through the back and found her in bed. Her throat had been slashed and there were stab wounds on her body. I went outside and phoned headquarters and waited. Then the cottage began to burn. I tried to at least get the body out of the bedroom for forensic analysis but the fire was too much for me.'

'You stupid loon,' raged Blair. 'The murderer must have still been in the hoose.'

'I saw and heard nobody,' said Hamish, wondering if he looked as stupid as he felt.

'Just you wait, laddie, until the boss hears about this.' Blair chuckled evilly. 'You'll be the first one who'll be suspected.'

To Hamish's horror, as the day wore on, a case seemed to be building up against him. There had been a tourist in the bar when Archie had talked about Hamish going to kill the witch, and he had told the police what he had overheard.

But despite Blair's pleas to Superintendent Daviot to arrest Hamish, he was blocked by the fact that Daviot descended on Lochdubh himself and began to interview the villagers. The milkman swore that he had called at the police station to report that Catriona's milk was lying outside his door and that he had followed Hamish a little way and was soon joined by other villagers. Hamish had emerged from the cottage after a few minutes and they had seen him phoning. Then the fire had started. Hamish had rushed into the cottage but then had run out calling to the crowd to fetch water.

'Did anyone fetch water?' Daviot asked.

Hughie, the milkman, hung his head and mumbled that they thought it a fitting end for the 'witch'.

So Daviot told Blair testily that Hamish had nothing to do with it and it seemed to him as if a bunch of superstitious villagers had ganged together to murder Catriona Beldame.

If the atmosphere in the village had been bad before, now it was worse with everyone feeling they were under suspicion.

Hamish worried and worried over the fact that he had not searched the cottage for anyone – had not even *sensed* the presence of anyone.

He phoned Jimmy. 'I've got nothing that can help you at the moment,' said Jimmy. 'Forensics have been working all day on what's left o' the place. There's one ray of sunshine.'

'What's that?'

'There's a new wee lassie on the forensic team. Keen as mustard. She's having an uphill battle wi' her beer-swilling, rugby-fanatical colleagues. But if there's anything to find, she'll find it.'

'Can you give me her name and home address?'

'Och, Hamish. Can't you just wait? It's just not the thing to call on a body at her home.'

'I cannae wait,' said Hamish. 'I feel like such an idiot.'

'I don't want to give her address. Try up at the witch's cottage. She might be still there.'

Hamish set out for the cottage. A great wind was tossing grey clouds over the sky. Buzzards wheeled above and a heron, its strong wings able to cope with the gale, sailed down and settled on a rock by the water.

Two television vans were already down on the waterfront, and he could see Blair's posse of policemen going door-to-door.

One policeman was on guard outside the cottage, hunched against the wind.

'Is there anyone from forensics still inside?' asked Hamish.

'Aye, there's a wee lassie from forensic.'

'I'll just be having a word with her.'

The policeman barred his way. 'Detective Chief Inspector Blair said nobody was to go in.'

'Aye, but he meant the press or the villagers,' said Hamish. He sidestepped round the policeman and went in, realizing suddenly that as he was visiting the scene of a crime, he should have been wearing his blue coveralls. He retreated to just inside the doorway and called out, 'Anybody here?'

A female voice called, 'I'm out the back.'

Hamish went out and walked around to the back of the cottage. He had a sudden vision of the type of female forensic investigator he had seen on American TV programmes – slim and tall with long hair and high cheekbones. So it came as something of a disappointment to see a small dumpy figure, covered in a white suit, white hood and white boots. She was searching diligently in the heather.

'Find anything?' asked Hamish. She stood up and pushed her hood back a little, revealing springy gold and red curls. Her cheeks were plump and rosy and she had large very blue eyes.

'Who are you?' she asked.

'Hamish Macbeth. I'm the local bobby. And you are . . .?'

'Lesley Seaton, forensics.'

'I came up here,' said Hamish, 'in the hope you might have found some reason for the cottage going up in flames. I found the body and then stood outside waiting for them from Strathbane to arrive. Then the cottage started to burn. What puzzles me is that I didnae sense anyone in the cottage.'

'I think I've found the reason for that,' said Lesley. 'I've found faint ash traces in the heather going a bit back. Some of the roots are scorched. It's my belief that someone lit a fuse.'

'Thank goodness for that,' said Hamish. 'I thought I was slipping. Wait a bit. I didnae smell petrol or anything like that.'

'I think – mind you, this is only a preliminary investigation – that the fuse ran into a plastic bucket of wastepaper placed under the wooden kitchen cupboards. I think the kitchen wall was soaked in some sort of cooking oil. I've only traces of things, mind you. Oil had been poured under the bed. The flames must have shot through the kitchen wall into the bedroom. There was a paraffin heater in the kitchen. That would add to the blaze, and then there was one in the bedroom as well.'

'Any idea when she was killed?'

'I'll need to wait for a report from the procurator fiscal,' said Lesley. 'It'll be hard to tell with the body being so badly burnt. But evidently there were two days' uncollected milk on the step, so maybe she was killed two days ago.'

'What I cannae understand,' said Hamish, 'is why then did the murderer wait so long to torch the place?'

'Maybe the murderer is some amateur who, once having murdered the woman, panicked. People see so many forensic programmes these days that they think someone will hold up a bit of hair a day later and say, "Aha, that's the DNA of Jock McHaggis", or whatever.' She sighed. 'Little do they know.'

'Where are the rest of your team?'

Her face hardened. 'They're playing Braikie at rugby tonight so they've all gone off to get ready. I've got most of my samples so I think I'll pack it in for tonight.' Her blue eyes twinkled. 'Am I wrong in thinking that Mr Blair is going to hate me when I produce evidence for this fuse? He's chortling and rubbing his hands and telling everyone who'll listen how Hamish Macbeth let a murderer get away from under his nose.'

'No, you're not wrong. I hope it was a long fuse.'

'Not very long. With this springy heather, it's hard to tell where it started but fortunately the back here is sheltered a bit from the wind. But farther away, the wind's whipped off any traces and I can't find any more scorched heather roots.'

'Let me go back and see if I can see anything.' Hamish got down on his knees and, starting at the point where she said she had found the ash, began to crawl off through the heather. To his relief, the wind suddenly dropped in that erratic way it has in Sutherland. He crawled past the markers she had laid out to map the track of the fuse and carried on after the markers had run out. The clouds were still racing across the sky. A fitful gleam of sunshine sparkled on something ahead of him in the heather. He crawled forwards and gently parted the heather. He found himself looking at two metal clothes pegs and a squashed glue stick. 'Come ower here and look at this,' he called.

She joined him. 'I didn't look far enough back. But I've an idea how the fuse could have been made.'

'How?'

'The recipe is one tablespoon of potassium nitrate, two to three spoonfuls of sugar, one glue stick, scissors, paper and a plastic zip-lock bag. You mix the sugar and the potassium nitrate in the bag, fold a long length of paper into a V, smear the valley of the V with the glue, clip the corner of the bag, and pour the contents into the V. Pinch together and twist and fasten either end with a clip until it all sticks.'

'So we're not looking for an amateur?'

'We still could be,' said Lesley.

'So where would an amateur buy potassium nitrate?'

'Off the Internet.'

'That's hopeful.' Hamish brightened. 'Anyone ordering the stuff would need to give a credit card number. They'd need to have a computer as well.'

'I shouldn't think a place like Lochdubh has many computers,' said Lesley.

'Oh, a whiles back, there were these writing classes and a lot of folks got one. Mind you, I think most of them will be gathering dust, but it's a start.'

Lesley gathered up the new evidence and put it in bags. 'It would be wonderful if I could get a print off any of this,' she said. 'I would also like the suggestion of a fuse leaked to the press.'

'Why?'

'Because a lot of your superstitious villagers think that either the fire was God's retribution or the devil had come to claim his own.'

'Why should we leak it to the press?'

'Because, if I am not mistaken, Blair will try to sit on this evidence. He still wants you as prime suspect.'

Hamish grinned. 'I know just the person. Would you be free for dinner tonight?'

'No, of course not. I've got to get this stuff back to the lab.'

'Oh, well . . .'

'But I'm free on Saturday.'

'Grand. Do you want to come here or Strathbane?'

'Just somewhere away from my gossipy colleagues.'

'There's the Glen Lodge Hotel, just north of Braikie. I could meet you there at eight.'

'Fine,' said Lesley. 'Now go and leak.'

Hamish felt guiltily that he should really give the story to the local reporter, Matthew Campbell. But there was his other reporter friend,

Elspeth Grant, who worked for a newspaper in Glasgow. Hamish had often thought of marrying Elspeth but something had always stopped him from proposing. He would not admit to himself that the something was the real love of his life, Priscilla Halburton-Smythe, daughter of the owner of the Tommel Castle Hotel, now working in London.

As he returned to the police station and phoned the newspaper in Glasgow, he half-expected to be told that Elspeth was already on her way to Lochdubh, but the news desk told him she was off sick.

He phoned her home number and a croaky voice he barely recognized as Elspeth's answered the phone. She said she had a fearsome cold and had missed out on the assignment to Lochdubh. Hamish wished her well and said he would phone again. He decided to ease his conscience and give the story to Matthew instead.

'And who do I say this came from?' asked Matthew when Hamish had finished telling him about the fuse.

'Chust say a source,' said Hamish, the sudden sibilance of his accent showing that he was feeling guilty.

'Right! This is great stuff,' said Matthew. 'I'll get it out to the nationals and TV.'

* * *

Blair hated Hamish Macbeth with a passion. He had previously enlisted the help of a prostitute to kidnap Hamish, hoping that in the policeman's unexplained absence he could persuade his bosses to put the Lochdubh police station up for sale. But Hamish had not only ruined his plot but also managed to get the prostitute into blackmailing him, Detective Chief Inspector Blair, to marry her. Not that any of his colleagues ever even guessed at his wife's rough background. After a few false starts, Mary Blair had modelled herself on Peter Daviot's wife, and there was no longer any trace of the prostitute in her manner or dress. Daviot was fond of telling Blair what a lucky man he was to have found such an excellent wife.

Before he switched on the television that evening, Blair was feeling quite kindly towards his wife. A glass of whisky had been waiting for him when he got home from work, his flat was clean and shining, and she had cooked him an excellent supper.

He switched on the television news, hoping to see film of himself because he had held an impromptu press conference on the waterfront. But when the news item about the murder of the witch came up on the screen, he saw it was not a picture of himself, but of Daviot, speaking to the press outside police headquarters.

He turned up the sound and Daviot's genteel accents filled the room. 'Yes,' he was saying, 'I have just received a report from the laboratory that the fire was set off by a fuse, which explains why the constable who found the body did not find anyone in the house.'

Mary looked over her knitting and saw her husband's face turn a nasty purplish colour with rage.

'Blood pressure!' she cautioned.

Jimmy Anderson called to see Hamish later that evening. 'Were you behind that leak to the papers?' he demanded.

'Would I dae a thing like that?' asked Hamish. 'Want a drink?'

'Aye. Blair is furious. But that local reporter insists he was up by the cottage and heard you talking to the forensic lassie.'

'So why blame me?' asked Hamish, all injured innocence.

'Just a hunch.'

'So what are the villagers saying?'

'Damn all. Except for a few of the more religious ones who think God sent down the fire to cleanse the place of her evil deeds. I asked Dr Brodie if any of his patients had come to him suffering from Spanish fly and he told me he couldn't discuss his patients. And not a man in the village will confess to having been to see her. Know anyone?'

'Not yet,' lied Hamish.

Jimmy's blue eyes had a shrewd look. 'I know you're a close-knit, loyal, superstitious community up here, Hamish, but a villager impeding the police in their inquiries is not nearly as serious as a copper doing the same thing.'

'Och, drink your whisky,' snapped Hamish. 'I'll see what I can find out. But what about her background? If she supplied iffy potions here, then it's ten to one she supplied them somewhere else. Was she ever married?'

'We're trying to find out.'

'Catriona Beldame won't have been her real name. Had she an account at the bank?'

'The bank manager says no, and any personal papers she had went up in the fire.'

'What if she changed her name by deed poll?'

'Still looking into that. But she bought the cottage! She paid cash.'

'How much?'

'Twenty-five thousand. Willie Ross, Sandy's brother, advertised the cottage in the paper. He says he was right glad to get the money because the place was beginning to fall to bits and no one wants a cottage with an iron roof and an outside toilet these days. All done privately.'

'What about stamp duty?'

'None required if it's under sixty thousand pounds. Look, Willie Ross badly needed the money. Along comes this Beldame female waving a fistful of notes at him, saying they didn't need to bother with lawyers. What was her accent?'

'Slight highland accent. Mind you, it's one of the easiest to mimic. I wish Elspeth were here.'

'Your ex-girlfriend? Why?'

'She's got a Gypsy background. I'm beginning to wonder whether Catriona was a Gypsy.'

'Fortunately Mr Patel at the grocery took a photo of her. He fancies himself as a cameraman. It's a good shot, full face. It'll be in all the newspapers tomorrow. Let's hope someone recognizes her.'

'I hope it turns out she's got some really nasty, ordinary criminal background,' said Hamish. 'That would stop this lot in the village thinking she was a witch.'

The picture of Catriona Beldame was featured on the front pages of nearly every newspaper in Britain. She had been photographed on the waterfront by Patel. It was a good clear shot of her standing in the sunlight.

Hamish, avoiding the press, set off to question people in the village. He started with

Willie Lamont, who was cleaning the restaurant preparatory to the lunchtime opening.

Willie loved cleaning. His Italian wife, Lucia, often complained that Willie's passion for new and better cleaning products took up too much space in their cottage.

He turned and saw Hamish and grinned. 'Wi' all these press folk, it's going to be busy,' he said.

Hamish removed his peaked cap and sat down at a table. 'Join me a moment,' he said. 'I want to ask you some questions about Catriona Beldame.'

'I don't want to talk about it,' said Willie defensively. 'I should never have gone to her, but Lucia hasn't been much interested in martial rights since the baby.'

Hamish wondered whether to correct Willie's malapropism but decided to let it go.

'I have to use a condominium,' said Willie, 'and that's no fun. Like having a bath with your socks on.'

'Isn't Lucia on the pill?' asked Hamish, momentarily diverted.

'She's a good Catholic.'

'So what happened when you saw Catriona?'

'She gave me some herbal tea and said to make sure Lucia took it, but Lucia wouldn't, so I went back to the witch and she said she could make my sexual progress –'

'Prowess,' corrected Hamish.

'Whatever. She said I would be irresistible but all I got was the itch. She caused a lot of misery in the village. Then men who went to her said there was no point getting all fired up if the missus wouldn't play. It's the older fellows in the village who were the most disappointed.'

'Like who?'

'I shouldnae say.'

'Come on, Willie, I'll find out anyway.'

'Well, there's Fergus Braid, him that works over at the paper mill, Archie, the fisherman, Colin Framont, the builder, and Timmy Teviot, the forestry worker. That's all I know about and don't you go saying you got it from me. Now I've got to get back to my cleaning.'

Hamish left in a haze of lavender-scented cleaner.

He decided to start with Archie. Archie was a friend. But he doubted whether the fisherman could tell him anything more than he had already. He went back to the police station first to let his dog and cat out for a walk up the fields at the back. He knew if he appeared with them on the waterfront, there would be tales about the eccentric policeman with a wild cat as a pet and Sonsie might be taken away from him.

The air had turned considerably colder. The loch was like black glass, the trees in the pine forest opposite reflected in the still water. The two mountains soaring above the village had snow on their peaks.

And in the midst of all this beauty, scurrying around or talking in little groups, were the press. Hamish longed for a quick solution to the murder so that he could get the village back again to its usual quiet ways.

Archie was sitting on the harbour wall in front of his cottage. Steam was billowing out of the open door of the cottage. His wife was a ferocious boiler of clothes, which perhaps explained why everything poor Archie wore always seemed too tight.

'Any news?' asked Archie.

'Nothing yet. I want you to tell me why you went to the witch in the first place and what exactly happened.'

'I went because o' my indigestion. Chronic, it is. Herself seemed right pleasant. She gave me some herb tea and it worked like a charm. She flirted with me, Hamish. Me! I knew herself had to be joking because she was a fine-looking woman and I'm no oil painting but it made me feel good – like a man again.

'I went back to get some more and herself started to talk about sex. Man, you know we don't talk about such things in Lochdubh. But with her pretty ways, she got me really fired up and she said she could sell me something that would make the wifie think I was great.'

'How much did she charge?'

Archie hung his head. 'Fifty pounds.'

Hamish was shocked. 'That's an awful lot o' money for you, Archie,' he said, 'what with the fishing being so bad.'

'I've never gone mad,' said Archie, 'but when I look back on it, it seems as if she drove me mad wi' –' his voice sank to a hoarse whisper – 'lust. Once I was a bit away from her, it all faded except for a wee bit o' my brain that longed to go back. Now I feel dirty. It's as if she scrambled up our minds, us men. It's like that wi' a lot o' the ither men. Women are a right funny breed. You see women on the telly just panting for a wee bit o' nookie, and the magazines telling them how to get the man in their lives excited. Och, well, the hard fact is we don't do sex in Lochdubh.'

'How do the other men cope?' asked Hamish.

'Just give up, like me, or they go to that br . . . Never mind.'

Hamish's hazel eyes sharpened and he pushed his peaked cap back on his fiery red hair. 'What were you about to say?'

'I wass about to say, or they go their own way.'

'I think you were about to say *brothel*. Where? Inverness? Strathbane?'

'I promised not to tell,' said Archie miserably. 'I gave my word and I'll not break it.'

Hamish gave up. He knew there were several brothels in Strathbane. What worried him was that one might have sprung up on his patch. It wasn't like the old days. Now women from Eastern European countries were being forced into prostitution.

His mobile phone rang. He glanced down at the screen and recognized Blair's home number. He was going to let it ring when he saw Blair standing outside the mobile police unit further down the waterfront. He realized it must be Blair's wife who was calling him.

'Hamish?' Mary Blair's voice came on the line. 'I need to talk to you but I don't want my old man to know about it. Can you come over?'

'I'll do my best, Mary, but I don't want your neighbours to see me and tell your husband. Meet me at Betty's café in the main street. None of the police go there. Say in about an hour.'

'Grand. It's important, Hamish.'

As it was Saturday, Hamish had hopes of finding the builder, Colin Framont, at home. He had torn down the old fishing cottage he had bought and replaced it with a bungalow with a fake Georgian portico made of wood at the front. Hamish thought it was lucky that Colin's monstrosity of a house was up at the back of the village instead of spoiling the front.

Colin answered the door. He was a heavy,

thickset man with grizzled hair, a beer paunch and watery brown eyes.

'Whit?' he demanded curtly.

'It's about Catriona Beldame,' said Hamish.

Colin's faded-looking wife, Tilly, joined him on the doorstep. 'Oh, Mr Macbeth,' she said. 'Would you like some tea?'

'No, he wouldnae like tea,' snarled Colin. 'Get back in the kitchen.'

When his wife had scurried off, Colin said defiantly, 'I only went tae her the once for indigestion pills.'

'There seems to be a fair amount of indigestion in Lochdubh,' said Hamish cynically. 'Can you tell me what she said?'

'She gave me some tea and I went off.'

And with that, Colin slammed the door in Hamish's face.

Hamish rang the bell again. No reply.

He banged on the door, which was swung open by a furious Colin.

'I've got naethin' mair to say to ye!' he howled.

'Look, we can either do things here or at the station,' said Hamish. 'Take your pick.'

To his surprise, the builder said, 'The station'll be fine.'

As they walked towards the police station, Colin said, 'I know what you want to ask but you cannae be asking things like that in front of the wife.'

In the station Hamish served him tea in the kitchen and got down to business. 'So what really happened?'

'It was around the men in the village that the witch could gie ye something tae make ye mair sexy to the wife, but the itch got so bad I went tae Dr Brodie and he told me it was dangerous stuff. I went up there to have it out with her but there was no reply.'

'When exactly did you go up to her cottage?'

'The day before she was found. I swear tae God that's the truth. You won't be saying anything to the missus?'

'No, on my word. Have you heard any talk about a brothel?'

'No, but if you hear of one, let me know!'

When Hamish entered the café in Strathbane, it was to find Mary Blair already waiting for him.

'So what's the news?' asked Hamish.

'You know that woman that was murdered,' said Mary. 'I think I met her.'

'Where? When?'

'I can't remember exactly but it was about two years ago. There was this woman – I'm not giving you her name – and she was on the game. Would you believe it? She was a married woman and did it for a lark. Said her man was tight with money. She wasn't on the streets like me. She had a wee flat that her husband didn't know about. All high class. Advertised herself on the Internet. She liked to talk to us prossies – seemed to get a kick out of it. Well, one day she stops by me. She'd been crying and looked like a real mess. She said she was pregnant and since she hadn't had sex with her husband in ages, he'd kill her if he found out.

'So I said why didn't she just go to the hospital and get an operation. Turns out her husband is a doctor and a member of the Rotary Club and the Freemasons and she said they all gossip and if she went for an abortion, it would get back to her husband. She said she'd heard of this woman who did abortions and she was going to her and she was right scared.

'I was sorry for her and said I would go with her. Mind you, I tried to talk her out of it. Back-street abortions were dangerous, I said. Anyway, we went out to a wee house on the Drumlie Road. She wasn't calling herself Catriona Beldame then. She was plain Mrs McBride. The place was clean and nice and I hoped it would be all right. She took my lady off to the bedroom. When they came out, this Mrs McBride said she would get her period like normal and abort and there would be no pain. I don't know what that woman did to her but she was found on the street, dead, a week later. She'd bled to death.'

'You should have gone to the police, Mary.'

'Me, a prostitute, going to the police and saying a respectable doctor's wife was on the game!'

'You could have written an anonymous letter.'

'And have forensics trace it back to me!'

'I doubt it,' said Hamish cynically.

'Anyway, I went back to that Mrs McBride to tell her she was a murderer, but the place was closed up and she'd gone.'

'Still, you've given me a starting point,' said Hamish, 'and you've also given me a motive for murder. What was the number of the house on Drumlie Road?'

'I can't remember, but it was about halfway along and had a yellow privet hedge in front of it.'

After promising Mary that he would not reveal where he had got his latest information from, Hamish left and phoned Jimmy Anderson.

When he had finished speaking, Jimmy said, 'I'll meet you in the car park at police headquarters and we'll go out to the Drumlie Road and see what we can find out.'

They found the house with the yellow privet hedge in front. The door was answered by a small, neat-looking middle-aged man. He volunteered that he was a Mr Southey and, yes, he had bought the house from Drummond's, the estate agent. The previous owner had been a Mr Tarrant.

'Not a Mrs McBride?' asked Hamish.

'No,' said Mr Southey. But he gathered that the house had been rented before he bought it.

Hamish and Jimmy got the address of Mr Tarrant from the estate agent. Mr Tarrant, said his wife who answered the door, was a solicitor and at his office. She gave them directions. Scottish advocates and solicitors are often, surprisingly, clever and charming, but Mr James Tarrant was like a lawyer out of Central Casting. He was plump and pompous with slightly protruding brown eyes and a pursed little mouth. His voice was high-pitched and querulous.

'Yes, I rented the house to Mrs McBride. Charming lady.'

'Do you still have the paperwork, her credentials and all that?' asked Jimmy.

He looked suddenly uncomfortable. 'I got rid of it all when we arranged the house sale.'

Hamish's eyes bored into him. 'You didn't ask, did you? She charmed you and paid cash.'

'She paid six months' cash in advance and I was glad to rent it.'

'When did she tell you she was leaving?' asked Jimmy.

'Well . . . er . . . she didn't. After the six months and there was no more rent, I called and found the place closed up.'

'Another dead end,' mourned Jimmy. 'You get back to Lochdubh and question the folks there and I'll go back to Drumlie Road and see if the neighbours know anything.'

Chapter Four

I expect that woman will be the last thing to be civilized by man.

– George Meredith

A small sun was shining through a thin veil of mist when Hamish returned to Lochdubh, creating that odd white light so typical of the north of Scotland. He could never quite get used to the mercurial changes of weather in his home county. It was hard to believe that a wind had ever blown across the still landscape. Everything was hushed and frozen as he got out of the Land Rover in front of the police station. No bird sang. There wasn't even anyone on the waterfront.

Hamish wondered where all the press had gone and why there was not even one sign of Blair and his policemen.

Then as he stood there, he realized how bitterly, bitingly cold it had become. He decided to collect his pets and set off to see the forestry worker before the mist became any thicker. He drove round the end of the loch, round to the other side, and stopped outside the forestry foreman's office. Hamish blessed the invention of mobile phones when the foreman rang Timmy Teviot and told him to come down to the office. It saved him from driving up the tracks, trying to find the man.

Timmy Teviot was small, thin and wiry with grizzled hair and a weather-beaten face. 'Let's step outside the office,' said Hamish. 'I've a few questions to ask you.'

Timmy followed him outside and lit up a cigarette. Hamish had a sudden sharp longing for one. He found it hard to believe that he had given up smoking some time ago.

'It's about Catriona Beldame, the murdered woman,' Hamish began.

'And what has that got to do with me?' demanded Timmy. His voice was soft and lilting.

'I believe you went to the woman for one of her potions.'

'Who's the wee gossip then?' demanded Timmy. 'I'll bet it was yon blabbermouth Willie Lamont.'

'Never you mind. I want to know what happened when you went to see her.'

'I went to see her for the indigestion . . .'

'Not again,' said Hamish. 'Out with it. What did you really go and see her for?'

Timmy sighed and sat down on a tree stump. 'I heard talk that she could make you like a stallion. But it didnae work and all I got was a visit to the doctor. I went back up there and asked for my money back. She laughed at me. Well, I'll be honest wi' ye, Hamish. I threatened her. She looked at me peculiar and said she'd put a curse on me. I'm telling you, I ran for my life. But I didn't kill her. I cannae stand up in court and give any evidence. If anyone got to hear of it, they'd laugh their heads off.'

'Do you know of anyone else who threatened her?'

'None of them want to talk about it. You don't when someone's made a right fool of ye.'

'Do you know anything about a brothel?'

'I wouldn't know about such things.'

Hamish dressed carefully that evening in his one good suit for his date with Lesley Seaton. He left in plenty of time, for the mist had thickened. As he drove slowly and cautiously towards Braikie, he began to worry about Lesley, motoring in this weather and maybe not being familiar with the road. He wished he'd taken a note of her mobile phone number.

By the time he arrived at the hotel, thick white frost had formed on the leaves of the rhododendrons on either side of the drive.

He was ushered into the hotel lounge to wait. A log fire was crackling up the chimney. To his relief, Lesley arrived five minutes later. She took off her heavy coat, revealing a plain black wool sweater and black corduroy trousers and serviceable boots. Her face was free of any make-up. Not hopeful signs, thought Hamish, who was always on the lookout for a new romance.

'So, any more news?' he asked as they walked into the dining room.

'Nothing much apart from a furious bollocking from Blair. He really does hate you. She had been viciously stabbed by someone in a rage. It's hard to pinpoint the exact time of death but from the report of the contents of her stomach, or rather what they could guess the contents were from a charred body, I guess it was sometime during the night and when she was asleep. There are no defensive wounds. I think it was the first stab that killed her, right in the heart.'

'I've been thinking about the fire,' said Hamish. 'At first I thought it was done in a last-minute panic to cover up any forensic evidence, but now I wonder. Potassium nitrate isn't just lying around. Someone had to have ordered it. Someone had to have got a key to the place somehow. I don't want it to turn out to be one of the villagers, but a lot of people still leave a key in the gutter above the door.

I do myself. Maybe someone knew about a spare key. Catriona was a stranger. She wouldn't think of searching in the gutter. Anyway, her name, last known was a Mrs McBride. She performed an illegal abortion on a woman who subsequently bled to death.'

'There's no need for back-street abortions these days,' said Lesley. 'Shall we order? The waiter's hovering and we're the only customers.'

It was a set menu. They ordered game soup, followed by roast rabbit and a bottle of Merlot.

When the waiter had left, Hamish said, 'It was evidently a doctor's wife who went on the game to make a bit of extra money. She was afraid her husband would find out, him being in the Freemasons and the Rotary Club. But it's a good motive for murder.'

'So you'd better find out who this doctor is.'

'Jimmy's working on it,' said Hamish.

He had to admit that she looked quite pretty in the soft lighting of the dining room. He wondered if she had a boyfriend. Maybe she was married! He judged her to be about the same thirty-something age as himself.

She was not wearing any rings but that might not mean anything. She would not wear rings when she was working.

'I just hope it doesn't turn out to be someone in the village,' said Hamish. 'Maybe she was married. Are you married yourself?'

'Was. Not now. The food here is very good.'

Recognizing a no-go area, Hamish ate steadily and then returned to discussing the case. 'It was really meant to look like a hate murder. And the fire . . . I wonder if someone really cold and calculating, and knowing about the superstition of the villagers, staged that fire when it would have the most effect.'

'You mean the wrath of God?'

'Or the devil come up from hell to take her home.'

'How can you live in such a place?'

'You are not a highlander, are you?' asked Hamish.

Those large blue eyes stared at him. 'What's that to do with it? I'm from Perth, actually.'

'Strange things do happen up here. I think it's to do with the rock. It's some of the oldest in the world and the soil on top is very thin. I sometimes think the ground in some places records strong feelings. You can go up some of the remote glens and get an overwhelming feeling of tragedy and then you find out that glen was the scene of a massacre after Culloden when the Duke of Cumberland's troops were not just routing the last of Prince Charlie's supporters but killing indiscriminately.'

'Fanciful,' she said briskly, 'but hard to believe.'

'Oh, it helps to keep an open mind. How are you getting on in your job?'

'Well. I don't drink to excess and I don't play rugby and I'm a female. They play silly tricks on me and it's getting wearisome. I'd like to see this case through to the end and then I think I'll get a transfer to Strathclyde.'

'Anything that could be described as sexual harassment?'

'Lots.'

'There you have them, lassie. Simply tell the lot of them that you are thinking of bringing a case of sexual harassment against them, and it'll amaze you how they back off.'

'I'll try that. Thanks. One thing puzzles me about the case. I would have thought it impossible to move about a village at any time of night without someone noticing.'

'I thought about that. Whoever it was could have approached the cottage from the back through the communal grazing ground.'

'Tell me a little about yourself,' said Lesley. 'Why aren't you married?'

'I'm choosy,' said Hamish. 'Let's talk about something else.'

Somehow the conversation became stilted after that. Hamish had been about to suggest they take their coffee through to the lounge in front of the fire but he suddenly missed the love of his life, Priscilla, with such a sharp pang that it amazed him. To Lesley's surprise, he quickly drank his coffee and called for the bill.

She found a sudden interest in this constable whom she had a few moments ago been privately damning as a local hick. He certainly was attractive-looking with his flaming-red hair and hazel eyes. And he must be well over six feet tall.

When they emerged from the hotel, it was to find the fog had lifted and an icy wind was blowing down from the mountains.

'My turn next time,' said Lesley.

'Aye, well, maybe when all this is over,' said Hamish. He walked her to her car, shook hands with her, and said goodnight.

Once back in the police station, he phoned Jimmy. 'Any news of that doctor?'

'Aye, we found him all right. We traced him through a report in the paper about his wife being found dead in the street. Reason for the death was all hushed up. He's a Dr Wilkinson, a general practitioner, and, get this, a friend of Daviot's.'

'Oh, my.'

'So we had to handle him with kid gloves. No getting him down to headquarters for a grilling. Daviot insists on handling it personally. But it seems to be a dead end. The doctor was off at a medical convention in Glasgow during the whole week covering the time she was murdered.'

'You can skip out of those conventions without anyone noticing,' said Hamish.

'Aye, well try telling that to Daviot. As far as he's concerned, the investigation into Wilkinson is finished and crawly Blair is going along with it.'

'I think it's got something to do with frustrated men,' said Hamish. 'Hear any talk about a brothel?'

'Just the usual ones in Strathbane.'

'I cannae see any of the villagers going to one of those,' said Hamish.

'Sometimes,' said Jimmy, 'a woman'll set up on her own. Do it on the quiet. Just a few customers.'

'If it's anywhere near Lochdubh, it'd need to be somewhere not overlooked,' said Hamish. 'Gossip would have spread around if a lot of different men were seen coming and going from a house.'

'Why are you so interested in a brothel, Hamish? It's got nothing to do with the case.'

'Unless it was someone to do with McBride or whatever her real name is. Also, I don't want to find one of those places where girls are tricked into coming over here from Eastern Europe and forced into prostitution.'

'Come on! They'd hardly set up shop in a godforsaken place like Sutherland.'

'Maybe.'

* * *

Hamish, going out to give his sheep their winter feed in the morning, found the ground covered with a light coating of snow. This was unusual, even for November. Because of the proximity of the Gulf Stream, Sutherland often escaped the harsher winters of central Scotland. Everything was still, grey and quiet.

He suddenly heard the phone ringing in the police station, breaking the silence of the morning. He paused for a moment, the feed bucket in his hand. Then he shrugged. He would check his messages in a moment. It was probably only Blair nagging him about something.

When he had finished feeding his sheep, he let his hens out of the henhouse and fed them as well.

Then he returned to the police station and made himself a cup of coffee before ambling through to the office to check his messages. Timmy Teviot's agitated voice sounded in the room. 'Hamish, it's me, Timmy. I've decided to tell you something I think you ought to know. I don't want anyone to see me talking to you. Could you ring me on my mobile?' He left Hamish the number and rang off.

Hamish rang immediately. In the past he had received calls from someone saying they had important information for him and that someone had ended up dead. But after a few rings Timmy answered. 'Could you meet me up at Rhian brae, just beyond the hotel by that big rock?'

'Can't you tell me now?' asked Hamish.

'No, later. At six o'clock when folks will be indoors having their tea.'

As he went out on his rounds, Hamish was relieved to see that a good number of the press had left. He decided to take a break from the case and call on some of the elderly residents in croft houses up in the hills to make sure they were all right, but all the time he was wondering what Timmy had to tell him.

Mr Patel, owner of the general store, was enjoying a quiet afternoon. The morning had been very busy but the fog had come down again, thick and clinging, and the villagers appeared to be staying at home. He had been up since dawn unloading and packing goods. He knew that to compete with the big supermarkets in Strathbane, he had to keep a large stock. He also allowed people on benefits to pay for their groceries at the end of each month when they received their government payments. He never threw away damaged goods but gave them away to pensioners.

The afternoon was quiet. He sat behind the counter, lulled by the warmth from a paraffin heater behind him. He was awakened by a terrible scream. He sat up with a jerk. Mrs Wellington was facing him, her face grey with shock. 'Get an ambulance!' she shrieked. 'Get the police.'

'What is it?' he cried, reaching for the phone.

'It's poor Ina Braid . . . blood all over her back. I think she's dead!'

Hamish received the call about Ina's murder just as he was about to head for his meeting with Timmy. He rang Timmy and told him what had happened, said he would phone him later, and rang off.

He raced towards Lochdubh, wondering who on earth would want to kill the inoffensive Ina Braid.

A small crowd, looking like ghostly wraiths in the thick mist, had gathered outside the shop when he drove up. Mr Patel was standing on the doorstep. 'Dr Brodie's with the body,' he said.

Sirens could be heard approaching from the direction of Strathbane. 'Who was in the shop?' asked Hamish.

'I wasnae aware of anyone,' said Mr Patel. 'I was tired and I must ha' nodded off. First thing I hear is this scream and Mrs Wellington shouting at me to call the ambulance and police. Och, Hamish, I feel sick.'

Before Hamish could ask any more questions, a car drove up and Blair got out. 'Another murder right under your nose, laddie?'

'I was out on my beat,' said Hamish.

'Out on my beat, what?'

'Out on my beat, *sir*.'

Blair pushed his way past Mr Patel and went into the shop. Hamish followed. Looking very small and crumpled in death, Ina Braid lay face-down on the shop floor in one of the two small aisles.

Dr Brodie straightened up. 'I suppose the pathologist will be here soon,' he said. 'Stabbed right in the back with something long and sharp. You know, sometimes when people have been stabbed, they just go on walking. She could have been stabbed somewhere else.'

'But she'd feel one hell of a sharp pain, not to mention the strength required to deliver the blow.'

'Not necessarily. It doesn't take much force to stab someone provided the point of the weapon is sharp enough. Just slides in, like stabbing a melon. Oh, here's Dr Forsythe.'

'I thought you had resigned,' said Hamish.

Before the pathologist could reply, Blair howled, 'Get outside and dinnae stand here gossiping. Someone must have seen someone going in to the shop.'

But there was trouble waiting for both of them when they exited the shop to find a furious Daviot staring at them. 'You pair! You went into the crime scene without any protective clothing.'

Blair cringed. 'Awfy sorry, sir. I had to get in there fast to make sure Macbeth wasn't messing up the crime scene.'

'I was outside the shop when you arrived,' protested Hamish.

'Don't just stand there, Macbeth,' said Daviot. 'Find out as quickly as you can who was in the shop with her.'

Hamish turned and addressed the crowd. 'Step forward anyone who saw Mrs Braid in the shop, saw her going into the shop, or saw her at all near the shop.'

Everyone began to edge away except a woman Hamish recognized as Tilly Framont. 'I saw her, Hamish,' she said.

Hamish led her away from the shop and took out his notebook. 'Where and when was this?'

She frowned with the effort of remembering. 'It would ha' been about five or ten minutes afore I heard the screaming. I didn't speak to her. Just nodded. She had a basket ower her arm and was hurrying towards the shop.'

'Was anyone else around?'

Tilly was a very small woman wearing a tight old-fashioned tweed coat with square shoulders. Her face had a sort of faded prettiness. She had a woollen hat pulled right down over her head.

'Let me see, Mrs Wellington was there talking to the Currie sisters. Archie Maclean was heading for the pub. There must have been other folks around but I couldn't really see, the mist was that thick.'

Hamish saw the Currie sisters retreating along the waterfront in the direction of their cottage. He excused himself, saying he would take a full statement from Tilly later, and hurried off after the sisters.

They heard him coming and swung round.

'You're not doing your job,' said Nessie.

'Doing your job,' echoed Jessie mournfully.

Hamish found it easier to shut out Jessie's constant echo of her sister's last words when he was talking to the twins. Their identical glasses were so thick as they looked up at him that he flinched a bit before two pairs of magnified eyes.

'Tilly Framont said she saw the pair of you on the waterfront just before Ina went into the shop.'

'That's right,' said Nessie. 'Oh, man, the pity o' it! There was herself as large as life. She gave us a cheery wave as she went past. Who did it? Must be that husband o' hers. He aye had a shifty look.'

'Did you see anyone following her?'

'No, it's right cold, you see, and the mist's awfy bad. Just the few of us, I think, but with the mist there could have been more people about. I saw Mrs Wellington. This is what they get for taking their mobile police unit away so soon. Let me see, there was that Archie Maclean going into the pub. Clarry Graham, the cook, was just standing there looking at the water, but I didn't really remark anyone in particular.'

Hamish thanked them and said he would talk to them later. He decided to go up to the Tommel Castle Hotel, where Clarry was a chef. In his brief glory days when Clarry had been Hamish's policeman, he'd been very inept – but maybe he had noticed something.

Clarry was just getting out of his battered old car when Hamish arrived at the hotel.

'What brings you, Hamish?' he hailed him. 'Priscilla's no' here.'

'I didn't come to see Priscilla,' snapped Hamish. 'Haven't you heard about the murder?'

'Aye, the wicked witch is dead.'

'No, not her! Just now. Ina Braid.'

'What's happened to this place?' said Clarry, his round face creased up like a baby about to cry. 'Such a nice wee body. It can't be that man o' hers. He'd never hurt a fly.'

'We'll see. I'm sure they've gone to pick him up. Clarry, you were seen down on the waterfront near Patel's. Who did you see?'

'I saw the Currie sisters and then Mrs Wellington. I wasn't really paying attention. Then the fog was so bad. I was thinking up a new recipe and I went for a wee walk to think better. I remember now that witch woman came up to the hotel one night for dinner.'

'Was she on her own?'

'Yes, she drank a lot and then began to complain about the food. She shut up when Johnson told her to pay her bill and get out or he'd call you.'

'What are the guests like? Anyone suspicious?'

'We've only got about six guests. It's quiet the now. But why don't you ask the boss?'

Mr Johnson was in the hotel office. 'What's all this I hear, Hamish?' he said. 'Ina Braid murdered!'

'It looks like that.'

'How was she killed?'

'It looks like a stab in the back.'

'It's that wretched Beldame woman. Somehow she's stirred up a lot of decent people.'

'I just hope it isnae someone in the village,' said Hamish. 'What about your guests?'

'They're all middle-aged to elderly and very respectable.'

'Could you print me out a list of their names and addresses?'

'Help yourself to coffee and I'll get it ready.'

Hamish left a few minutes later, studying the names and addresses. He would run them all through the police computer, but he hadn't much hope of finding a villain amongst the lot of them.

He drove back to Lochdubh, parked on the waterfront, walked up to the builder's house, and then slowly began to walk back the way Ina would have taken on her road to the shop.

The way led down a narrow lane between the cottages, bordered by fences and hedges. He looked to right and left. Someone could easily have stood in the narrow lane, waiting for Ina. Say the weapon *was* thin and sharp. But surely she would have felt something – turned around and seen her assailant. And would she just have gone on walking, determined to do her shopping? The fog was dense in the lane. Maybe she felt the stab, turned around and saw no one, and kept on walking. He began to call at the cottages whose gardens bordered on to the lane, but no one had seen or heard anything.

When he got back to the waterfront, the police mobile unit was back in place. Hamish blessed his wild cat. Had Blair not been so terrified of the cat then he would have commandeered the police station.

He saw Jimmy Anderson outside the unit

and went to speak to him. 'They're bringing Fergus in, Hamish,' said Jimmy.

'From the paper mill?'

'No, the man was out fishing. He had the day off. Blair all but charged him with murdering his wife but then fell into a passion when the water bailiff turns up and says he was talking to Fergus and sharing a sandwich with him all around the time they estimate his wife was being murdered.'

'How long until the pathology report?' asked Hamish.

'Dr Forsyth's working on it. I don't know. These things take time.'

'If she was stabbed and went on walking,' said Hamish, 'then it probably happened in the lane down from her house to the waterfront, but, och, surely she would have turned round and screamed or something. Not just gone ahead to the shop.'

'Patel says he dozed off. Someone may have nipped into the shop and stabbed her.'

'I hate that idea,' said Hamish moodily. 'That might mean it was someone from the village that people were so used to seeing, it didn't really register. Then with this damn fog, it could have been anyone.'

'Blair's got coppers going from door to door. But you know these people. What sort of a person was Ina Braid?'

'Quiet sort of woman. Just one of the village

women I occasionally spoke to. I barely knew her because there was never any trouble either with her or Fergus. No children.'

'Who's the biggest gossip in the village?'

'Gossips,' corrected Hamish. 'The Currie twins. I've already spoken to them. Nothing there. Wait a bit. I've had an idea. There's a back way into the shop!'

'I'll get along there and tell forensics. That lassie you've been romancing, Lesley Seaton, is working there.'

Hamish blushed. 'I have not been romancing Lesley Seaton!'

'Well, you were seen having dinner with her up at the Glen Lodge Hotel.'

'Isn't that chust typical?' said Hamish furiously. 'No one sees a damn thing when a wee woman is being murdered under their noses but I take a colleague out for dinner in an empty dining room miles outside the village and immediately everyone knows about it.'

'You're Lochdubh's famous bachelor, Hamish. Anytime you're seen with a woman, it's a first-class piece o' gossip.'

Hamish suddenly remembered Timmy Teviot. He wondered what the forestry worker had wanted to tell him that was so secret he had to meet him outside the village.

'I've got someone to see,' said Hamish. 'Look, Jimmy, do me a favour. The minute you get anything from Dr Forsythe, let me know.'

'I'll do that if I can with Blair breathing down my neck.' Behind him, the mobile unit dipped and swayed. 'Here he comes. You'd better be off.'

Hamish hurried back along the waterfront. Timmy, he knew, shared lodgings with several other forestry workers in caravans on the other side of the loch. He got into his Land Rover and drove off.

He located Timmy's caravan by dint of knocking on other caravan doors and asking where Timmy lived.

Timmy answered the door, and his face fell when he saw Hamish.

'I'm right sorry I brought ye all the way here on such a cold night,' said Timmy.

'Yes, it is cold, so ask me in?'

'I've got company,' said Timmy, looking nervously behind him.

'And who would that be?'

'It's just a lassie who minds the bar in Braikie.'

'All right. Step outside and talk to me.'

Timmy reluctantly came down the caravan steps. 'I feel a fool, Hamish. It's really nothing now I think of it. I saw a couple of deer poachers up on the hill.'

'So what was so private about that?'

'Thae deer poachers can be vicious. I didn't want any of them to see me going to the station. They saw me watching them.'

Hamish took out his notebook. 'Where?'

'Up on Brechie moor. Two big fellows, one with a beard, a short grey beard. Must ha' been middle-aged. The other was young. Could ha' been his son. Tall thin laddie wearing a wool cap like the older one. They had dark green shooting jackets and both were carrying deer rifles.'

Hamish studied Timmy's face in the light shining from the caravan window. 'And did one of them have a scar on his face?' he asked.

'Now you come to mention it . . .'

'Timmy, you're telling me a bunch o' lies. What was it you really wanted to tell me?'

'I'm telling you the truth, I swear.'

'Your eyes tell me you're lying.'

'That would make a good song, Hamish,' said Timmy. 'Got to get back to business.' He nipped quickly into his caravan and slammed the door.

Hamish remembered that Colin Framont and his wife, Tilly, lived next door to the Braids. Perhaps they could give him some details about Ina Braid's life and whether she had made any enemies.

Tilly answered the door to him. 'Come ben,

Hamish,' she cried. 'Isn't it awful. Poor Ina who wouldn't hurt a fly.'

Hamish removed his peaked cap and followed her into the living room, where her husband was watching television. He rose when he saw Hamish and switched the television off.

The living room was neat and clean. Almost too uncomfortably clean, thought Hamish.

'I wonder if you, Tilly, could tell me what sort of a person Ina was,' began Hamish. 'I never really knew her that well.'

'Very quiet,' said Tilly.

'Did she and her husband ever quarrel?'

'Never a cross word.'

'That's going a bit far, Tilly. All married couples surely quarrel sometimes.'

'Yes, but not violent. I mean I never heard any shouting or yelling. Besides, if there had been anything like that, Ina would have told me.'

'I keep wondering whether it had anything to do with the death of the woman who called herself Catriona Beldame.'

'It could be,' said Tilly. 'I mean, there could be some maniac on the loose. The police have been in her house, searching it from end to end. Poor Fergus. He must be heartbroken. They took him away for questioning. They must be mad.'

'He should be back soon,' said Hamish. 'It seems he has an alibi.'

'Oh, that's grand, isn't it, Colin?'

'Aye,' said Colin. 'I'll give him a knock and get him in here for a drink.'

Hamish asked more questions, but they did not seem to have anything interesting to say.

When Hamish began to walk down the lane, he saw a tall figure silhouetted by the lights from the waterfront. The fog had thinned to a slight haze.

'Is that yourself, Fergus?' he called.

'Yes, it's me, Hamish.' His voice broke on a sob. 'That bastard Blair. I could kill him!'

'Hush, now. Don't let anyone hear you saying things like that. I'll walk you back to your house. Do you want me to go and get you a dram?'

'I've got a bottle in the house. Come back wi' me, Hamish. I feel a wreck.'

Housekeeping in Lochdubh, thought Hamish as he looked around the living room in Fergus's cottage, was not a chore but a religion. It was so clean, it looked sterile.

He took off his cap and sat down as Fergus took a bottle of whisky from the sideboard along with two glasses and poured a couple of drinks.

Fergus settled back in an armchair and looked moodily at the fireplace. He took out a packet of cigarettes and lit one. 'Who on earth would kill Ina?' he said. 'I can't get it into my head that she's dead. I keep expecting her to walk into this room any moment.'

'Your ash is about to drop on the carpet,' said Hamish. 'Can I get you an ashtray?'

'None in the house,' said Fergus, flicking the ash into the fireplace. 'Ina was allergic to cigarette smoke.'

'I have to ask you this, Fergus. Could she have been seeing another man?'

'What? Ina? Man, who'd even look at her?'

'That's a wee bit harsh.'

'Well, she wasn't a beauty, that's for sure.'

The doorbell rang. 'I know who that is,' said Fergus. 'It's them next door. Could you go and tell them that after I answer police questions I'm going straight to bed?'

Sure enough, Tilly was standing on the doorstep holding a casserole. She listened to Hamish making his excuses for Fergus and then handed him the casserole. 'It's a good lamb stew,' she said. 'You tell him I'll be round first thing in the morning to pick up his laundry and do his cleaning.'

Hamish took the casserole in and placed it in the gleaming kitchen. 'I heard what she said,' said Fergus when Hamish joined him. 'I won't answer the door.'

'So, Fergus,' said Hamish patiently, 'rack your brains. Did Ina have any enemies?'

'No.'

'Did she have anything to do with Catriona Beldame?'

'No, I mean she wouldn't.'

'She might have gone there for something like a love potion.'

'What for? Me? Ah, well, you're not married, are you?'

Hamish continued to question him. He asked if there were any letters he could see but Fergus shook his head and said they hadn't a computer, either.

Hamish at last rose. He turned in the doorway. Fergus was studying a TV guide. 'Man, there's American football on tonight,' he crowed.

There's a man who looks as if he's just been let out of prison rather than having lost a wife, thought Hamish.

Chapter Five

Kissing don't last! Cookery do.
– George Meredith

Hamish was surprised when he returned to the police station to find not one single hectoring message from Blair on his answering service. Then he decided that it was because the detective chief inspector wanted to keep both murder cases firmly to himself.

Jimmy came in after him without knocking and sat down at the kitchen table with a sigh.

'What a day!'

'Got any background on Catriona?'

'A bit. She was married to a Rory McBride, crofter of Inverness. Maiden name was Catriona Burrell.'

'On the police records?'

'Nearly but not quite.'

'What do you mean?'

'Gimme a whisky and I'll tell you.'

'One of these days,' said Hamish, lifting

down a bottle of whisky from a kitchen cupboard, 'Blair's going to die of acute alcoholism and you'll find a hellfire teetotaller is your new boss. Probably a woman. And she'll have you in rehab as fast as anything.'

'When Blair pushes off, I'll get his job. I'm practising my funny handshake already.'

'You're never going to join the Masons!'

'If it was good enough for Rabbie Burns, it's good enough for me. Just joking.'

'So,' said Hamish as Jimmy took a first gulp of whisky, 'tell me what you meant about Catriona.'

'She was in Drumnadrochit not long after her separation, right down at the end of Loch Ness. Police got a rumour she was pushing drugs – Ecstasy. Two detectives got a search warrant and went along. One of them phones in to say they've found a stash of the stuff and they're bringing her in. An hour later, the other one phones back and said they'd made a mistake and there were no drugs in the cottage at all.'

'Who are these detectives?'

'Detective Sergeant Paul Simmonds and Detective Constable Peter Lyon.'

'Odd.'

'Wait a bit. There's more. You're going to love this. Although the cottage is a bit isolated, folks walking back to the local hotel said they heard the noise of a party going on. Lights shining, music blaring. Then two men staggered out and one shouts back, "See you soon, Catriona." The men answered the descriptions of the two detectives. A waitress at the hotel was walking to her evening shift as well. Evidently her husband had been visiting Catriona and she was jealous. So she phoned it in. More police were sent but there wasn't a drug to be found although they took that cottage apart. Shortly after that, Catriona disappeared.'

'And what happened to the detectives?'

'Suspended from duty pending an inquiry. Nothing found against them. Simmonds is now working as a security guard in Glasgow and Lyon got a transfer to Edinburgh.'

'She could hardly have had much custom to peddle drugs in a wee place like Drumnadrochit,' said Hamish.

'There was a rumour she had been seen at a couple of the clubs in Inverness. I'm telling you, Hamish, wi' a woman like that, anyone out of her past could have had it in for her.'

'I hope it is someone from her past,' said Hamish.

'What's this? You've cracked at last and think one of your precious peasants could be a murderer?'

'Let's hope not.'

After Jimmy had left, Hamish was wondering what to eat. He had frozen food in the freezer out in the shed in the garden but he didn't feel like defrosting anything. There was a knock at the door.

He was half-tempted to ignore it, fearing Blair had decided that some Hamish baiting was called for, but after a short hesitation, he opened it and found Lesley on the doorstep carrying a large pot.

She seemed almost shy, and avoiding his gaze she said, 'I made too much beef stew and I wondered if you would like some.'

'Bring it in,' said Hamish. 'Have you eaten?'

'Not yet.'

'Then we'll have our dinner together. The stove's hot. Just put the pot on top.'

'Right. I've got some wine in the car.'

'Now, is this wise?' Hamish asked Lugs. 'But that stew smells wonderful.' Lesley came back brandishing a bottle, which she put on the table. Hamish helped her off with her coat. She was wearing a lime-green woollen dress that clung to her ample curves.

'So how are things going?' asked Hamish.

She pulled a flowered pinafore out of her capacious handbag and put it on. She went to the stove and began to stir the stew. When did I last see a woman under sixty in a pinafore? wondered Hamish. And oh, the aroma of that stew! Was anything ever more seductive than a curvaceous woman in a pinny bent over a stove?

'As you've probably already been told, the

weapon used was something very thin and sharp. Although she was wearing a tweed coat, it would not take all that much force. It was driven straight through her back and pierced her heart.'

'But could she have gone on walking after being stabbed?'

'Not in this case. I think she died instantly and in the shop. I gather the thick fog is the trouble. Someone could easily have followed her in and got out again quickly and the fact that Patel was asleep was a bonus.'

'But why her?' asked Hamish, laying out plates, knives and forks and then searching for wine glasses. 'I can understand someone wanting to kill Catriona. She seems to have been a right evil woman.'

'Say this Ina Baird knew something and had to be silenced,' suggested Lesley. 'The stew's hot enough. Pass me the plates.'

'I don't like that idea,' said Hamish. 'Not a bit.'

'Why?'

'If Catriona was murdered by someone from her past, he wouldn't hang around the village. Your idea makes it look like someone local.'

Lesley dished out the stew and they ate in silence, Hamish relishing every delicious morsel.

When they had finished eating, she collected the plates and put them in the sink. 'Back in a minute,' she said. 'I've got the dessert and coffee in the car.'

Refusing Hamish's offer of help, she went out and then returned carrying a cheesecake on a plate and a thermos of coffee.

'You're spoiling me, lassie,' said Hamish.

'It's the least I can do after that meal you bought me,' said Lesley. 'My God! What's that?'

Sonsie appeared in the kitchen and stood glaring.

'Oh, that's my cat. Nothing to worry about. Yes, it's a wild cat. Harmless.'

Lugs came back into the kitchen and sat beside the cat.

'There's some stew left,' said Lesley. 'Do you think they would like some?'

'I'm sure they would.'

Lesley filled up the animals' feed bowls with stew. How pretty she looks, thought Hamish, mellowed with food and wine.

'What made you want to be a policeman in a remote place like this?' asked Lesley. 'And I've heard gossip about how you keep side-stepping promotion.'

'It goes a long way back,' said Hamish. 'I was a lad in my early teens. Patel's shop was a greengrocer's then but it was going bust. Not much call for fresh vegetables in Lochdubh and folk grew pretty much all they needed. So the owner was selling everything off cheap. My mother drove me over. It was a scorching hot summer day and we only had an ancient

Land Rover with a cracked radiator and we had to keep stopping on the road to fill it up with water.

'My mother bought a lot of stuff and we loaded it in the Land Rover. Then she said she would go and visit a friend. I said I'd stay and look at the boats in the harbour. She gave me a couple of pounds and told me that the greengrocer's was selling off boxes of plums at a pound each. She'd decided to buy some after all. She suddenly wanted to make plum jam. So she gave me the car keys and told me to buy a couple of boxes.

'She had just gone when an ice cream van came along the waterfront. I was so hot and thirsty and I craved an ice cream. I bought a large one and hid the change in my shoe.

'I was sure she would understand but when she came back and started talking about all the plum jam she was going to make, I panicked and lied. I knew we were pretty poor and we weren't allowed luxuries like ice cream. I said two youths had attacked me and taken the money.'

Hamish sighed. 'It was misery. She marched me to this police station. It was a Constable McWhirter, a big slow-moving highlander. I told my story and he just sat there, studying my face. Then he said, "Take off your shoes, laddie."

'I blustered and argued but I had to take my shoes off. He shook them and the change came rattling out. My mother gave me a tongue lashing but McWhirter said, "I think the lad has learned a good lesson. Crime doesn't pay. I swear he'll never do anything like that again."

'That policeman seemed like God to me, and I loved Lochdubh. As soon as I left school, I went through police academy and got a job in Strathbane. But as soon as I heard that McWhirter had died – they had trouble finding anyone for the job up here – I volunteered. I've never wanted to be anywhere else. What about you? Why forsensics?'

'I've always been fascinated by forensic science. But that was what broke up my marriage. I was working for Strathclyde and there was an enormous workload. I was hardly ever home. He said it was either the job or him, not both. I chose the job.'

'But why Strathbane?'

'I was silly enough to have an affair with a colleague. It got messy. I had to get out. I don't really want to talk about it.'

There was a long silence. She poured them cups of coffee from a thermos.

'It's frustrating,' said Hamish at last.

'What is?'

'Being out of the loop. Not having all the facts as they come in.'

'That was your choice, remember?'

'Aye, I suppose I want to run the case without the responsibility of rank,' said Hamish.

While they finished their coffee, Hamish wondered what he was supposed to do now. Invite her to stay the night?

But she suddenly stood up. She said abruptly, 'I'll call back sometime for the cheesecake plate and the stew pot. I'll take the thermos because I use that for work. Goodnight.'

'Wait a minute,' said Hamish, uncoiling his long legs from under the table. 'This has been a fabulous meal. I must take you out for dinner.'

'I'll phone you,' said Lesley, and with that she fled out the door.

Hamish scratched his fiery hair. His animals looked sleepily up at him.

'What brought that on?' said Hamish.

Lesley got into her car and drove off. A slight wind was shifting the fog into bewildering pillars of mist floating in front of the car. 'Fool!' she told herself. 'He may be attractive but you're not destined to spend the rest of your life stuck in a highland police station.'

In the Highlands of Sutherland it's possible to get three climates in one day. When Hamish arose the following morning it was to find the fog had cleared, leaving a damp, warm blustery day with choppy waves on the loch and a feeling almost of spring in the air. But he knew from experience that it could be freezing again by the evening.

He cleaned up the dishes from the night before, putting the stew pot and the dessert dish to one side to return to Lesley.

Hamish went along in the direction of the mobile police unit and then backed off. A line of villagers, all men, were queuing up outside.

He stopped a Strathbane policeman who was moodily smoking a cigarette and staring at the water.

'What's happening?' asked Hamish.

'The boss is getting the DNA of all the men in this village,' said the policeman. His accent had the fluting sound of the Outer Hebrides.

'That won't do him any good,' said Hamish. 'As far as I know no DNA was recovered from the scene.'

'Aye, well, they are going to look at the DNA database.'

'Why didn't they ask me?' asked Hamish. 'I could have told them no one in this village has a criminal record.'

The policeman tossed his cigarette butt on to the beach. 'I had best be getting on. But I'm right sick o' rapping at doors and asking hard-faced wifies what their man was doing when that Braid woman was getting herself killt.'

Hamish stood, irresolute. Before, Blair would have been shouting at him to do something or other. But he had no instructions. This time Blair seemed determined to keep him right out of the case.

He took out his phone and called Jimmy. 'Can you speak?'

'I'm at headquarters making calls.'

'Can you tell me where Paul Simmonds is working in Glasgow?'

'You can't go there, Hamish. Your expenses wouldn't be paid. Besides, you'd be seen as poaching on Strathclyde's police territory.'

'Would I do a thing like that? Chust for interest.'

'Oh, well, he's working at Wylie's, a big sort of Harrods-type store in Buchanan Street.'

Hamish told his pets to look after themselves. He felt he didn't dare inflict them on Angela again. He drove rapidly to Inverness airport and caught the shuttle to Glasgow. He had changed into civilian clothes.

Glasgow was freezing cold. The balmy air, blessing Sutherland when he left, had not reached south.

Hamish shivered his way along Buchanan Street until he came to Wylie's.

A member of the staff informed him that the security guard was off on his coffee break and could be found in the shop's café in the basement.

The café was quiet, but Hamish spotted a middle-aged man in dark blue coveralls with a badge proclaiming security on the front. Paul Simmonds was small for an ex-detective and plump, with a discontented face covered in red veins. His eyes were faded blue and watery.

Hamish sat down opposite him and introduced himself.

'What now?' snarled Simmonds. 'If it's about that woman what got murdered, I've answered all the police questions I'm going to answer.'

'Come on,' coaxed Hamish. 'This is unofficial. I'm not out to blame you for anything. I want to know what the woman last calling herself Catriona was like.'

Paul stared into his coffee cup. Then he raised his head. 'You're not wearing a wire, are you?'

'I'm here at my own expense and my boss would kill me if he found out.'

'You're that Hamish Macbeth from Lochdubh, aren't you?'

'The same.'

'Well, I've heard nothing but good about you. I suppose there's no harm in telling you. I'm out of the force. I think she really was a witch. Yes. We had her bang to rights. Found a bag of Ecstasy tablets. I phoned over the find. She didn't seem the least put out. Just smiled and said, "Let's drink to success." It was a bottle of twelve-year-old malt. I was all for hauling her off but Peter said it wouldn't hurt to have just the one drink. I don't know what was in that drink but I suddenly felt happier than I'd done in my whole life. The fire was crackling on the hearth and the room was cosy what with the wind howling outside down the loch.

'Suddenly she looked beautiful. "We'll have a party!" she cried, and somehow there we were singing and dancing. It was all a blur. Then she kissed us both goodnight, and when we were halfway to Inverness we came to our senses and searched for the evidence. It was gone and in that moment, we realized we hadn't even arrested her. We went back but the place was in darkness and she didn't answer the door. We tried to break it down because we still had the warrant, but the door was too tough for us and man, we were still drunk and shaky.

'Then came the inquiry. They cleared us of any wrong-doing but it was on our records and we knew we'd never get any promotion after that. I'm right glad she's dead and I hope she suffered.'

'And was she using her maiden name of Catriona Burrell?'

'Yes. Look, if you catch whoever killed her, shake his hand from me.'

'When you were searching the house for drugs, can you remember anything else; letters, postcards, photos, things like that?'

'Let me think. I know, Peter picked up a framed photograph and says, "Do you think her man's still around?" I only had a wee keek at it, mind, but it was of a big strong fellow and written at the bottom was FROM YOUR LOVING HUSBAND, RORY.'

'That's grand,' said Hamish. 'Anything else?'

He sat for a few minutes in thought. Then a voice from the tannoy barked, 'Security guard, report to the main entrance.'

Hamish handed over his card. 'If you remember anything at all, phone me.'

Simmonds got to his feet. 'I 'member now. Behind the fellow was a view of a harbour. It looked like Oban.'

When Hamish reached Inverness airport, before getting into his old car, he phoned Mr Johnson at the Tommel Castle Hotel. 'Do me a favour,' said Hamish. 'If Blair phones you, tell him I was up at the hotel all day checking on the guests.'

Mr Johnson agreed. Hamish drove off towards Lochdubh, feeling that at least he had covered himself in case the erratic Blair had suddenly decided to hound him.

As he drove back, he turned over in his mind what Simmonds had said. If Catriona had married this Rory, then it might be worthwhile to go to Oban and look for a Rory McBride.

Jimmy Anderson was waiting for him. 'I thought you might be back soon. Have you anything for me because I'm right tired of getting nowhere.'

Hamish led him into the kitchen and told him what he had found out.

'I thought,' said Hamish, 'if you'd cover for me, I might take a run over to Oban in the morning and see what I can find out.'

'I'll think of something if there's any whisky left.'

'One, Jimmy, only one. I don't want you to be done for drunk driving.'

When Hamish put the bottle and a glass on the table, Jimmy filled the glass up to the brim and took a swig. 'That's better. Blair's been worse than ever. Mike Haggerty, thon foreman who gave Fergus Braid an alibi, well, Blair's decided they're in cahoots and Mike is lying. Mike's in the cells at the moment.'

'Why?'

'He shouted, "Are you calling me a liar?" Blair said yes, so Mike socked him on the nose. But I think Mike will be out by now.'

'Why?'

'Because Mike's sister, Shona, is a advocate who lives in Dingwall, and she's demanding to hear a tape of the interview and screaming police harassment. Daviot told Blair to let her hear the tape and wouldn't you know it, Blair hadn't got the interview recorded so he's in deep poo.'

'Let's hope that keeps him quiet for a time,' said Hamish. 'He was always awful about badgering and arresting the innocent, but I swear he's getting worse.'

'Aye, that's the drink for you,' said Jimmy, taking another hearty swig from his glass.

Hamish drove down to Oban the following morning, taking the cat and dog with him. He sometimes thought the pair were worse than children, having to be regularly watered and fed. At least Sonsie's company meant that Lugs would roam far and wide with the cat up on the moors and manage to consume quite a large amount of food without getting fat.

The day grew darker as Hamish drove south into Ross and Cromarty. Oban was a pretty place in the summer but as he drove down to the waterfront, a gale was whipping across the harbour. He asked about Rory McBride in various shops, pubs and restaurants along the waterfront but without meeting any success.

He then went up to the offices of the local newspaper, the *Oban Journal*, and asked to see the editor.

The editor listened to his request and then asked a reporter, Isla Damper, to go with Hamish and search the files. Isla was a tall thin girl with thick glasses and a spotty face. Her unfortunate appearance was redeemed by a soft highland voice, a charming smile and beautiful large brown eyes flecked with gold.

'I'll try the weddings first,' she said, going to a large filing cabinet. 'We're putting everything on computer disks but it's a long slow job and Wee Geordie who's supposed to be doing the job went off to Thailand two months ago and hasn't come back. The best thing is to look in the photo file. If this Rory McBride wasn't local then there might just be a photo and caption.'

She searched diligently, puffing on a cigarette. 'I thought smoking was banned in offices in Scotland,' said Hamish.

'Aye, well, there's offices and offices.'

After an hour of searching, she sighed. 'You know, I should just put the mannie's name up on the computer.'

She sat down at a computer and switched it on. Hamish could see the early northern night coming down outside the window, where a seagull looked in at him with contempt before flying off.

'Got something!' she cried. Hamish unwound himself from the typing chair he had been sitting on and looked over her shoulder. 'There was a photo,' she said, 'but not under marriages.'

The photograph showed Catriona and Rory McBride on the waterfront. 'On their honeymoon in Oban, happy couple Rory McBride and his wife, Catriona.'

'Can you give me a copy of that photograph?' asked Hamish.

'If I can find it.'

'Try under Catriona McBride.'

'Okay.'

She tapped away busily. Then she said, 'Our cross-referencing leaves a lot to be desired. Here we are. But it's about him. That photo was taken four years ago in July. Now here we are, still in the same July, and Rory McBride is appealing for any sighting of his missing wife.' There was the same photograph of the couple to illustrate the news item. Rory McBride was described as a crofter from Torgormack outside Beauly in Inverness-shire. He and Catriona had come to Oban to spend their honeymoon. In the middle of the second week, she had disappeared, but as she had taken her belongings with her, Hamish gathered the police were not really looking very hard for her.

He looked at his watch, trying to calculate how long it would take him to get to Torgormack and see if he could find Rory McBride.

He thanked Isla and left, stopping on the waterfront to buy a fresh fish for Sonsie, haggis-and-chips for himself, and a hamburger for Lugs. They all sat in the Land Rover, eating in companionable silence. Hamish wondered whether to leave going to try to find the crofter until the next day or he could phone Jimmy and get the Inverness police on to it. But he decided he wanted to see the man for himself. He also wondered if Strathbane had found out anything about Catriona Burrell's background.

* * *

The little crofting community at Torgormack seemed quite prosperous – a few trim bungalows instead of old croft houses. By knocking at the nearest door he got directions to Rory McBride's address.

It was further up the hill from the other houses and had a run-down appearance.

Hamish rang the bell. He could hear no sound of ringing inside and so he knocked on the door. A man he barely recognized from the photograph as Rory McBride answered the door. He looked much older and careworn.

Hamish introduced himself and said he was looking into the death of Catriona.

'Oh, her,' said Rory wearily. 'You'd best come in.'

The living room was bleak with only a few bits of old furniture. A peat fire smouldered on the hearth, sending out very little heat.

'I'm surprised you didn't contact the police when you learned of her murder,' said Hamish.

'Sit down. A dram?'

'I'm driving,' said Hamish. 'Your marriage didn't seem to last long.'

'No.'

'How did you meet her?'

'I met her at the game fair down in Perth. I was fair bowled over. She was staying in Perth at the time.'

'I'll need that address.'

'I've got it somewhere,' he said wearily. 'I'll look for it in a minute.'

'Go on.'

'It was a whirlwind romance. I proposed right away. I stayed at her place and then we got married in Perth and went to Oban on our honeymoon. I suppose it was my fault. I told her I was a farmer. I wanted to impress her. She started asking questions about the farm when we were in Oban. That's when I told her I was a crofter. She stared at me and she exclaimed, "A croft? One of those tiny small-holdings?" I said I had eighteen acres and kept sheep. She went a bit quiet after that. She started going off for long walks on her own.

'Then one day I came back and she'd packed up and gone. I reported her disappearance to the police. They weren't inclined to bother because she had taken her luggage with her. Also, she had cleaned out my wallet but somehow I couldn't tell them that. Then someone said they had seen her getting into a fish lorry, which headed off out of the town in the middle of the night.'

'Did you never try to find her?'

'I did for a bit. I went back to her place in Perth but there was a new tenant there. I just gave up. It was obvious she had married me because she had thought I was a rich farmer.'

'I'm afraid you're now going to have detectives calling on you,' said Hamish. 'It'll look to them as if you had a reason to murder.

Where were you the day she was killed? That's estimated to have been during the night on the tenth.'

'Here.'

'Anyone see you?'

'On the evening of the tenth I was down at a dance in the Lovat Arms Hotel. I didn't leave until one in the morning.'

Still time to drive like hell to Lochdubh, thought Hamish, but as if reading his thoughts, Rory said, 'And in case you're thinking I drove up there afterwards, my Land Rover was off the road for repairs and I went down to Beauly in the tractor.'

'When you were staying at her place in Perth, were there any photographs? Did she talk about her family?'

'No, come to think of it. She gave the impression she'd been an only child. I told her all about my family, about my brother in Dubai and my sister in Hong Kong. In fact, I did most of the talking. I don't remember seeing any photographs.'

'How much money did she steal from you?'

'A little under two thousand pounds.'

'What?'

'Aye, you see, just before the Perth game show, I'd won five thousand pounds on a lottery scratch card. I was so tired of scrimping and saving. I wanted to have some fun. I got myself new clothes, I flashed money around at that game show. No wonder she thought I was rich.'

'But you didn't tell her about the scratch card, did you?'

He hung his head. 'I wanted to impress her. I was frightened if she knew the real truth then she wouldn't marry me. Well, that's hindsight. I think I only suspected that deep down.'

'See if you can find that address in Perth for me.'

'I remember it was Petry Road, the bottom half of a Victorian villa, but I'll find the street number for you.'

Hamish felt sorry for him and was glad the man seemed to have a good alibi.

Rory came back. 'It was number twenty-four A.'

Hamish thanked him and left. It was too late now to go to Perth and he wondered if he dare take any time off the next day.

Chapter Six

Still obscurely fighting the lost fight of virtue, still clinging, in the brothel or on the scaffold, to some rag of honour, the poor jewel of their souls!

– Robert Louis Stevenson

'Now we're in trouble!' howled Jimmy when Hamish phoned him the following morning. 'Inverness police are to interview McBride today and they'll find out you've been there before them. Couldn't you just have left it to them? I'd have let you know what they found out. I'll try to make excuses for you and keep this from Blair but don't you dare go near that Perth address. I'll let you know what the Perth police find out.'

Hamish went out on his rounds. He called to question Timmy Teviot again but the forestry worker stuck doggedly to his story about poachers.

In the evening Jimmy phoned. Catriona Burrell's mother, Morag, had been a Gypsy who had abandoned Catriona shortly after the baby was born. She had been brought up by her father, a strict lay minister in the Methodist Church. He had died when their home had gone up in flames one night when Catriona was seventeen. Arson was suspected but nothing was ever proved. Catriona was moved into the care of her father's sister, Agnes, a few streets away from the burnt home. When Catriona was eighteen, Agnes had died after a fall down the stairs. She had inherited her brother's money on his death, and that money then went to Catriona.

'How much?' asked Hamish.

'Altogether with the insurance from the fire and then the sale of Agnes's house plus the money old Burrell left, about three hundred and fifty thousand pounds.'

'Worth killing for,' said Hamish. 'Didn't the police think Agnes's death suspicious?'

'She was older than her brother, in her late sixties, and crippled with arthritis. The death wasn't considered suspicious.'

'And where was Catriona at the time of the fire?'

'In the house. She was rescued from an upstairs bedroom window by a fireman. Burrell didn't get out.'

'And when the aunt died, where was she?'

'She was out in the centre of Perth with friends. Of course, they couldn't pinpoint the exact time of death.'

'I'd be willing to bet she bumped off both of them,' said Hamish. 'Now, was there any other relative who might have felt cheated out of the inheritance?'

'No, but there was one furious wee woman, a widow, a Mrs Ruby Connachie. She had been stepping out with Burrell and had hopes of marrying him. She hated Catriona with a passion. At the time, she told the police that Catriona had set the fire.'

'What was the source of the fire?'

'A chip pan.'

'Who cooks chips in the middle of the night?'

'Catriona said that her father cooked all the meals. This seems to have been true. He fancied himself a nutritionist. Catriona said they had fish-and-chips for tea and her father must have left the gas on low under the chip pan. From the remains of the cooker, they estimated that seemed to be the case. Sister Agnes said she was surprised because Horace Burrell, her brother, only cooked healthy food and never fried anything. So perhaps our witch left the pan on deliberately until it hotted up and burst into flames. There's another curious thing. Ruby Connachie had had a tour of the house with the view to becoming the next Mrs

Burrell. She swore Burrell had a lock on his bedroom door, but no remains of a lock were found although the door was burnt to cinders. I wonder if Catriona locked him in and threw away the key.'

'They would look for the lock, surely.'

'Ruby only came out with all of this after the death of Agnes. The fire was quickly put down as an accident. The bedroom floor had collapsed in flames before the firemen could save it. All Catriona had to do was wait, go into the ruin when the investigation was over, and find the thing.'

'So what's this Ruby like?'

'Churchgoing, God-fearing wee body. She said Catriona was the "devil's spawn".'

'Looks as if she might be right,' said Hamish gloomily. 'Whoever killed Catriona hated her. And that fire could have been retribution rather than to cover up any forensic evidence. What's this Ruby's alibi?'

'She lives alone. She was certainly seen out and about in Perth, shopping, visiting the church, that sort of thing. She could have driven up during the night. She's got a car.'

'What's her alibi for the time the fire was lit at the witch's cottage?'

There was a rustling of papers. Then Jimmy said, 'Nobody asked her. I'll phone Perth and tell them to get on to it right away.'

'The way Catriona went on,' said Hamish, 'the whole of Scotland's probably littered wi' folks who wanted to murder her.'

'You sound quite cheerful about it. Glad suspicion's moving away from the local teuchters?'

'Not at all,' said Hamish. Although he knew Jimmy was right.

But Timmy Teviot knew something and he wasn't talking. Hamish decided to order him to come to the police station and make a full statement about the poachers.

Timmy turned up that evening. Try as he would to trip him up, Hamish found that Timmy stuck unwaveringly to his original story.

Hamish was to say later that not only did the case go cold, it went into deep freeze. On the day that there was a march in Strathbane against global warming, blizzards hurled down from the north, blanketing the country-side. Most of the protesters had come in from other parts of the country and soon found themselves stranded.

The snow piled up, blocking the highland roads despite the diligence of the snow ploughs. At Christmas, Lochdubh looked like an old-fashioned Christmas card with candle-light shining at the cottage windows because there had been a massive power cut. During a break in the storms, Hamish used snowshoes to visit the outlying crofts. Two weeks into the new year, and the snow was still falling.

In his kitchen, Lesley's stew pot and cake plate lay as a mute reminder that she had never come back to collect them and that, before the snow, he had not even tried to contact her.

He suddenly remembered the brothel idea. He got out an ordnance survey map and began to mark off locations in easy reach of Lochdubh where someone could run a brothel without alerting the neighbours. The spirit of John Knox still gripped parts of the north, and he was sure if it had been a large business, he would have heard of it. Someone would have reported it.

It would not, he thought, be an isolated croft house up on the moors because crofting neighbours would have reported something to him. When they were out with their sheep, they saw everything in the landscape that moved.

Then if men from Lochdubh had been visiting it, it would need to be somewhere quite close.

Perhaps Angus Macdonald, the seer, knew something. Hamish was very cynical about the seer's psychic powers but knew that Angus collected a good deal of useful gossip.

Also, he realized, he should call on Angus

anyway. The man must be in his seventies and might be in need of food.

Hamish went to Patel's and filled up a haversack with powdered milk – there had been no deliveries of fresh milk – locally baked bread, butter, cheese, tea and coffee. Putting on his snowshoes and hoisting the haversack on his back, he set off to climb the hill at the back to Angus's cottage.

To his alarm, there was no answer to his knock at the door. He tried the handle and found the door unlocked. He walked in, calling, 'Angus!'

He heard a faint croak from the bedroom and opened the door. Angus was huddled in bed. The room was freezing.

'What's up, Angus?' asked Hamish, bending over him.

'I think it's the flu, Hamish. Dr Brodie came up. He said it was a bad cold and left me some pills to take my temperature down.'

'I'll get a fire going in this bedroom for a start,' said Hamish.

He worked busily, lighting a fire and then, in the kitchen, preparing a bowl of soup and some toast and carrying the lot in on a tray to Angus. He propped the seer up on his pillows and placed the tray in front of him. 'Try to get that down you,' said Hamish, 'and I'll make you some tea afterwards. You shouldnae be alone like this.'

Hamish retreated into the kitchen and phoned Mrs Wellington. After he had made Angus tea and persuaded him to take some aspirin, Hamish heard approaching voices and went to the front door.

There was nothing in the world, he thought, more indomitable than the ladies of Lochdubh. Fighting their way up the hill came Mrs Wellington, the Currie sisters and Angela. Angela was pulling a laden sledge.

Soon the little cottage was a hive of activity. Angus was persuaded to move through to his living room wrapped in blankets and sit by the fire until the sheets on his bed were changed.

'You're a kind man, Hamish,' croaked Angus.

Hamish looked quickly around and then bent over Angus. 'Know anything about a brothel near Lochdubh?'

'You wouldnae be punishing a wee body for doing a few men a favour,' he wheezed.

'Not me. But where?'

Mrs Wellington came in. 'I hope you are not bothering our patient, Hamish. We need more peat for the fire. And get out the back and knock the snow off his satellite dish so he can watch the telly.'

'I didn't know you had satellite television, Angus,' said Hamish.

'Stop bothering the man,' boomed Mrs Wellington, 'and get to it!'

Hamish collected more peat from a shed at

the back. Then he got a ladder and climbed up to the satellite dish – which was on a pole – and cleared the snow from it. He felt the wind on his cheek and realized it had moved round to the west. The snow had stopped falling, and there was a little patch of blue sky appearing above his head.

When he went into the bedroom, the television had flickered into life. The Currie sisters were sitting on either side of the fire, drying their feet.

'The Misses Currie are going to stay with Angus for a bit. I'll call up this evening,' said Mrs Wellington. 'Oh, the thought of that walk back.'

'I'm taking the sledge back,' said Angela. 'We could sledge down the hill along the track we made coming up.'

'You'll never get me on a sledge,' protested the minister's wife, but once outside, she quailed at the thought of struggling all the way down.

'Hamish,' said Angus. 'Come near.'

Hamish bent over him.

'Cnothan. Mobile home. Up on the north brae.'

'Come along, Hamish,' ordered Mrs Wellington.

Outside, Angela and a reluctant Mrs Wellington sat on the sledge. Hamish pushed from the back and jumped on board and they all went hurtling down, ending in a heap against a garden fence at the bottom.

'That actually was fun,' said Mrs Wellington, standing up and brushing snow from her clothes.

The thaw came quickly the following day, only to be followed by a sharp frost turning the roads treacherous. Hamish got a call from gamekeeper Willie. 'There's a couple o' fellows skidded off the road up north of the hotel.'

'I'll see to it,' said Hamish.

A gritting lorry was making its way along the waterfront, spraying sand and salt. Hamish followed it out of the village and up the hill past the hotel to where two men were standing on the road, talking to Willie. Their Land Rover was lying on its side in the ditch.

Hamish got down and approached them. He stared. The older man had a beard and was accompanied by a younger man. He nodded to them and said to Willie, who was standing with his gun broken, 'Get your shotgun on them.' To the two men he said, 'Don't dare move.'

He took two sets of handcuffs out of his own vehicle and handcuffed both men, who were protesting violently. He then went to their Land Rover and peered inside. A deer carcass was lying in the back. So Timmy wasn't lying after all, he thought.

By the time he had taken them down to the police station, locked them in the one cell, phoned Strathbane, and filed a report, the ice on the roads had melted and a squad arrived from Strathbane to impound the poachers' vehicle and take them to Strathbane. From their driving licences, he identified them as Walter Wills and Granger Home.

As they were led off, the older man turned and spat at Hamish. 'You're a dead man,' he said.

That evening, the weather remained relatively mild and the air was full of the melted snow, dripping from roofs. Hamish planned to set out the next morning to Cnothan.

He once again looked at the stew pot and plate. If the weather stayed mild, then he might run over to Strathbane and return both to Lesley. He was surprised that she hadn't contacted him. On the other hand, he should at least have sent her a note or some flowers to thank her for the meal. He sat down at his computer, contacted Interflora, and ordered a bunch of spring flowers from the Channel Islands to be sent to her. He hesitated over the message and finally wrote, 'Thank you for a splendid dinner, Hamish.'

That being done, he began to write out all he knew about the murders of Catriona and Ina to get it clear in his head. The fact that the back door of Catriona's cottage did not appear to have been forced pointed to a local who might have known where a spare key was kept. On the other hand, it had been a simple Yale lock, easily sprung with a credit card.

Every time he thought of Catriona, he felt rage building up inside him. He was sure she had been a murderess. He wished he could get down to Perth but Jimmy would get to hear of it and Hamish did not want to lose his friend. At least Blair had been quiet. As soon as a case went cold, Blair quickly concentrated on other cases, often building them out of proportion so that Daviot would hopefully forget about the murders.

His mind ranged over the men in the village. There had been no odd incomers. He knew them all. He checked into the police records of the guests who had been staying at the hotel, but they all had impeccable backgrounds. What of Ruby Connachie in Perth, who must have felt she had been cheated out of a cosy marriage? Jimmy had filed all the reports. Maybe he had incorporated the Perth interviews. To his relief, Jimmy had filed the interview with Ruby. Hamish looked dismally at her age. Ruby was now seventy-six years old. She was a staunch member of the Methodist Church. Her statement was full of hatred for Catriona. She said it was God's punishment. On the day of Ina's death and at the very time they estimated Ina was being murdered in Patel's grocery store, Ruby had been having lunch in Perth with two old friends. Hamish read and reread all the reports until he realized it was late at night and he wanted to get off to Cnothan in the morning early.

Great pools of melted snow lay along the waterfront as he drove off in the morning with a brisk breeze sending little waves across their surfaces. A pale sun rode high in the washed-out blue of the sky. 'I wish I could see Elspeth again,' he said over his shoulder to his pets in the back.

'There he goes, talking to himself again,' said Nessie Currie, watching as the police Land Rover disappeared over the bridge at the end of the village. 'That man needs a woman in his life.'

'Woman in his life,' echoed Jessie.

Hamish drove to Cnothan and then up the brae to the north. He could see no sign of a mobile home so he stopped at one of the outlying crofts.

'Do you know if there's a woman living in a mobile home near here?' he asked a gnome-like man who answered the door of the croft house.

'Herself has gone,' said the crofter. 'It wass chust afore the snow. Big truck moved the whole thing. Tellt someone she was moving ower to Bonar Bridge.'

Hamish thanked him and started off on the road to Bonar Bridge. When he got there, diligent questioning gave him the information that there was a mobile home parked on the riverbank a bit outside the village.

Bonar Bridge has a long history dating from the early Bronze Age settlements. The locals call it Bona, probably from part of its Gaelic name, Drochaid a Bhanna.

After an hour of searching, he found a mobile home, screened by trees, on a grassy bank of the river. An old Rover was parked outside.

He knocked at the door. There was no reply. He tried several times. He turned the door handle. The door swung open. The smell that met him made his heart sink. He went back to where he had parked his Land Rover and put on his blue coveralls and overboots and then donned a pair of plastic gloves. He went back to the mobile home, where the door swung back and forth in the breeze. He went inside.

There was a double bed at the end of the mobile home, and on that bed lay a plump grey-haired woman, her dead eyes staring and her chest covered with dried blood. He stepped outside and phoned Strathbane. Then he went back in again and began to carefully search around. In a drawer, he found a passport. Her name had been Fiona McNulty, aged fifty-five. Along with the passport was a cheque book and various receipts for bottled gas, food and drink. Under the receipts was a typed note. It read, 'You're next, you whore. I'm coming for you.'

He went back outside and up to his Land Rover. He took out a picnic basket and fed the dog and cat and filled their water bowls. He had a cup of coffee from his thermos but he didn't feel like eating anything. What on earth, if anything, could connect the dead woman with Ina Braid and Catriona? And this dead woman, Fiona McNulty, certainly did not look like a prostitute.

It seemed to take a long time for the squad to arrive from Strathbane but finally they were all assembled: pathologist, forensic team, Jimmy, and, at the head of it all, a furious Blair, knowing that Daviot would now be on his back for having not persevered in solving the first two murders.

Hamish gave his report and was told by Blair to go and start knocking at doors in Bonar Bridge. Lesley had turned up with the forensic team but she had not once looked at him. Waste of flowers, thought the ever-thrifty Hamish sourly.

Hamish knew more policemen would soon be knocking on doors as well, and he wanted to get ahead of the pack.

An elderly lady inhabited the nearest cottage. She invited Hamish into her neat parlour and exclaimed in shock over the murder. 'Such a decent lady,' she mourned. 'What's your name, young man?'

'I'm Hamish Macbeth from Lochdubh,' said Hamish, taking out his notebook. 'And you are?'

'Mrs Euphemia Cathcart.'

'You are English?'

'Yes. My husband was from Bonar and we moved up here when we got married. He's been dead these twenty years. You sit there and I'll make some tea.'

Hamish waited until she came back with a laden tray. He brightened. Not only tea but also homemade scones. He was suddenly hungry.

'Did you know the dead woman?' he asked.

'Yes, I did. She was so nice and kind. She would fetch me stuff from the shops occasionally and drop in for a chat. She was from Glasgow but she said she liked the Highlands and when her husband died, she bought that trailer thing and moved up here. She said when she got tired of a place, she could move on. Of course her old car couldn't pull that great thing but she said there was always someone locally with a truck to do it for her.'

'I don't want to shock you, Mrs Cathcart, but there was talk of her being a prostitute.'

'I am shocked. The malicious things people

do say. She was a decent lady. One of the best. We became friends right away. I really will miss her. It was probably a poaching gang. They're vicious, those salmon poachers.'

'But you never saw any men going near her home?'

'Not a one. Don't you listen to that rubbish. The bad side to some of the highlanders is that they will make up stories.'

'Did she talk about anyone or did she say she had recently been parked over near Cnothan?'

'No, come to think of it, apart from telling me about her young days in Glasgow, she didn't mention the last place she'd been.'

'And do you know if she was friendly with anyone apart from you?'

'I'm sure there was bound to be someone but she never said . . . Oh, God! It's horrible!' She pointed with a shaking finger at the window.

Blair's face, swollen with booze and contorted with anger, was glaring through the glass.

'It's all right,' said Hamish soothingly. 'It's chust the boss.'

He went to the door and opened it.

'Whit the hell dae ye think ye're doing, sitting there on yer arse drinking tea?' howled Blair.

'Mrs Cathcart here was a friend of the deceased,' said Hamish.

Daviot loomed up behind Blair. 'What is going on?' he demanded.

Blair swung round. 'I was just asking Macbeth here what he thought he was doing drinking tea with some auld biddy.'

A gentle reproving voice from the doorway said, 'I do not like being called an auld biddy. I have just been telling this nice policeman that the poor dear Mrs McNulty was a friend of mine. You,' she said, glaring at Blair, 'are a good example of why people in this country have lost respect for the police.'

Daviot stepped forward. 'I am sure the chief inspector did not mean to insult you. Please carry on, Macbeth.'

Hamish followed Mrs Cathcart back indoors. 'I think I've actually got enough for the moment,' he said.

'Just you sit down and finish your tea. It must be horrible working for a man like that.'

'Just one more thing,' said Hamish. 'May I have another scone?'

'As many as you like.'

'Thanks. What I really meant to ask was, did you ever go along to the shops with her?'

'I went the once.'

'Did she seem to be particularly friendly with any of the shopkeepers?'

'I remember there was a Mr Tumulty at the craftshop. She seemed to be on good terms with him.'

'I'll try there.'

'Drop by anytime.'

Mr Tumulty was a small, faded-looking man dressed entirely in grey. He had grey hair and grey watery eyes in a pale face. Hamish judged him to be in his fifties. The news of the murder had spread like wildfire. 'This is terrible,' he burst out when Hamish entered the dark little shop. 'Who would want to murder poor Fiona?'

'I gather you were friendly with her.'

'We got talking when she came in to buy one of my mohair stoles. She invited me back to her home for supper one night and I had a nice time. I escorted her to the kirk one Sunday. We've got a rare fine minister.'

'I have to ask you this, sir,' said Hamish. 'Did you know that Mrs McNulty was suspected of being a prostitute?'

'Never! A more respectable lady you could not wish to meet. That's a nasty slander.'

'I'll leave that for the moment. Did she seem to be frightened of anyone?'

'No.'

'When did you last see her?'

'I can't exactly remember: I phoned her several times but I didn't get a reply.'

'On her mobile?'

'Yes.'

'I'll maybe get back to you.'

Hamish went outside the shop and called Jimmy. 'I didn't see a mobile phone in her place,' he said. 'Can you get the men to look for it? If we knew who'd been phoning her, that would be a great help. And did she have a computer?'

'I'll get them on to it. Getting anywhere?'

'The two people I've talked to so far think she was the epitome of respectability,' said Hamish. 'What gets me is if she was on the game, how did she advertise?'

For the rest of the day, Hamish trudged from door to door until he was weary. At last he joined his grumbling animals in the police Land Rover and set out for Lochdubh after checking with Jimmy.

He stopped halfway there and let them out for a run. The weather had turned cold again and he shivered as he walked up and down, waiting for the dog and cat to come back.

He eventually got them back by rattling their feed bowls. 'You've been fed already today,' he grumbled, 'but if you're good, I'll find you something when we get home.'

As Hamish drove along the waterfront of Lochdubh, he suddenly stopped the Land

Rover and stared ahead at the police station. It was a clear starry night, and he could see smoke rising from his chimney.

If someone wanted to ambush me, he thought, they'd hardly go to the trouble of lighting the fire. He drove on and parked outside. The kitchen light was on.

The door was unlocked. He opened it and went inside.

Elspeth Grant was sitting at his kitchen table. Hamish felt a sudden surge of gladness. She looked more like the old Elspeth than the citified one she had become recently. Her hair was frizzy and formed a halo round her face. Her peculiar silvery eyes looked at him seriously. She was wearing a black cashmere sweater over black corduroy trousers and black suede boots.

'Who's dead?' asked Hamish.

'I came to ask you that. This murder over at Bonar. I went straight there but I couldn't find you.'

'I meant the black clothes.'

'I was sent up here in a hurry, and put on the first things that came to hand.' The cat let out a slow hiss and Lugs glared up at her.

'I see your two wives are as jealous as ever,' said Elspeth.

'Just cut that out,' said Hamish. 'I'd forgotten what a nasty piece of work you could be.'

'Simmer down. You've forgotten what a help I can be.' She fished in a bag at her feet and produced a bottle of whisky. 'Want a dram?'

'I could do with one.' Hamish sat down with a sigh. 'Then I need to eat something.'

'Have a glass and then I'll take you to the Italian restaurant.'

'Can I take Lugs and Sonsie with us? They'll give them something in the kitchen. And don't look at me in that pitying way.'

'Sure. Bring them by all means.' Elspeth opened the bottle as Hamish put two glasses on the table. She poured them each a generous measure.

There was a knock at the kitchen door. 'If that's my photographer, get rid of him,' said Elspeth. 'He's the world's worst bore.'

But it was Lesley. 'I came to get my pot and plate,' she said. 'Oh, you've got company.'

Hamish made the introductions. 'A reporter!' exclaimed Lesley. 'You should know better than speak to the press.'

'We're old friends,' said Elspeth. 'And Hamish knows I never use anything without his permission.'

Lesley stood awkwardly. 'Anyway, I came to pick up my things and thank you for the flowers. They were beautiful.'

Elspeth wished she would go away. But her innate highland courtesy, combined with the fact that this was a forensic expert who might have some interesting details, prompted her to say, 'I was just about to take Hamish out for dinner. Why don't you join us?'

'I don't want to barge in . . .'

'It's all right. Give her a glass, Hamish, and then when we finish our drinks, we'll walk along to the restaurant.'

Over an excellent meal, Lesley listened as Hamish began to talk about the three murders. It was a concise and intelligent report. Lesley felt a stab of irritation that such an obviously intelligent man should waste his talents stuck in a highland village. Of course, if he married the right sort of woman, she would drum some sense into his head.

Then she became aware that Elspeth's eyes were surveying her. And those eyes seemed to be saying, *I know exactly what you're thinking*. To her fury, Lesley found herself blushing. She rose to her feet. 'Got to go to the loo.'

'Hamish, oh Hamish,' teased Elspeth when they were alone. 'She plans to marry you and make you over.'

'Stop havering, Elspeth, and turn your mind to these murders. What do you think?'

'There doesn't seem to be anything to connect them. If Fiona McNulty was on the game, then that sort of life can lead to violence and her death may not be connected to the others.

Catriona seems to have made so many enemies, it's hard to know where to start. Now, it's the one in the middle that fascinates me – Ina Braid.'

'Why her?'

'Think about it. Here's a decent God-fearing woman, hardly a murderee. So she must have known something. It stands to reason. So the thing to do is to ask and ask and see if she said something to anyone. I feel she *must* have said something and if she did whoever she talked to might be too frightened to say anything. She must be part of the first murder, but I can't see any reason for the murder at Bonar.'

Lesley rejoined them. 'We've just been discussing the murders,' said Hamish. 'Any idea when Fiona McNulty was killed?'

'About four or five days ago at a guess. Someone must have battled their way through the snow to get to her. The mobile home's parked on heather so there's no hope of getting a footprint. Everything in the trailer had been wiped clean. Not even a spare hair.'

'Do you know if they found a mobile phone?'

'No sign of one.'

'Anything off that threatening note?'

'What threatening note?' asked Elspeth.

'Someone called her a whore and told her she'd be next.'

'We're working on it. It was written on a

computer,' said Lesley. 'But whoever wrote it used gloves.'

'No sign of a weapon?' asked Hamish.

'No, but it was not the same weapon that killed Ina Braid. This was as if it had been done with something like a hunting knife. The stab wounds on Catriona's body were made with something with a serrated edge, like a bread knife.'

Hamish suddenly wanted to be alone with Elspeth.

'I think you should be getting on your way, Lesley,' he said. 'The weather's changing and you don't want to be caught in a blizzard.'

Lesley looked from one to the other and then got up and put on her coat. Hamish walked with her to the door of the restaurant. 'Goodnight,' he said firmly. She looked past him to where Elspeth was sitting watching them and then she stood on tiptoe and planted a kiss on Hamish's cheek, said breathlessly, 'I'll phone you,' and hurried off into the night.

Chapter Seven

The mair they talk I'm kent the better.
– Robert Burns

'What if,' said Elspeth when Hamish returned and sat down, 'the murder of Fiona McNulty has nothing to do with the other two? She was a woman living alone in a trailer. Some passing maniac might have wanted money for drink or drugs. Was she sexually assaulted? And was there any money in the mobile home?'

'I'm slipping,' said Hamish ruefully. 'I'll phone Jimmy.'

Jimmy answered and asked, 'Where are you?'

'I'm in the Italian restaurant.'

'Be with you in a minute. I'm along at the station.'

Hamish rang off and said, 'Jimmy's in Lochdubh. He'll be with us in a few minutes.'

Jimmy arrived and shrugged off his coat. 'Man, I'm famished.'

'Join us,' said Elspeth. 'I can entertain the police on my expenses.'

'As long as you don't go printing anything you shouldn't. Willie!' he called to the waiter. 'Get me a bowl of spag bol and a bottle o' plonk.'

'We dinnae serve plonk,' said Willie.

'Well, something red wi' alcohol in it.' He turned to Hamish. 'Man, I'm tired. Give me a bed for the night?'

'Yes, but you're not getting any of my clean underwear. Jimmy, was the Fiona woman sexually assaulted?'

'According to the first brief examination, no.'

'Was there any money taken? Any valuables?'

'Not that anyone could see. Her handbag was in a cupboard with all her credit cards and two hundred and ten pounds in cash. There was a gold wedding ring on one finger and a diamond ring as well. She had a wee TV in the living area. That hadn't been taken. So robbery wasn't the motive.'

'That's a pity,' said Hamish.

'Why?'

'I've a feeling that if the motive had been robbery, that might have been one less murder to solve. That would have suggested a villain, and we could have checked up with people with a criminal record on the database. It looks awfy like this one was connected to the others. Is there anything in Ina Braid's background that might lead someone to kill her? She's been in the village as long as most folks can remember. Churchgoing, member of the Mothers' Union, absolutely blameless.'

'Fergus Braid in his interview said they had been married for twenty-eight years. Both local. Met at a ceilidh. Ina was working as a secretary over at Braikie. Got married and Ina became a housewife. End of story.'

'She must have known *something*,' said Elspeth. 'I've got to do a colour piece. I'll go around the village tomorrow speaking to people. They all know me and they'll talk to me easier than they would even to Hamish.'

Hamish felt suddenly uneasy. 'Remember, there's a murderer out there, Elspeth. Don't go putting yourself in danger.'

'I'll be careful.'

Hamish awoke the next morning to the sound of a gale hammering at the building. He sniffed. There was a nasty smell of stale booze and sweat that even the many draughts in the police station couldn't dispel. Then he remembered Jimmy was sleeping in the cell.

He got up, washed and dressed, and roused a protesting Jimmy. He put out a glass of water and a packet of Alka-Seltzer on the kitchen table – Jimmy's usual breakfast. He went into the bathroom and ran a hot bath. Jimmy was sitting on the edge of the bed, groaning.

'I've run a bath for you,' said Hamish.

'I don't want a bath.'

'Yes, you do. You stink. Get to it!'

Hamish retreated to the kitchen, where he made a pot of strong coffee. Jimmy eventually emerged. He dropped two Alka-Seltzer tablets into the glass of water and then drank it.

'I don't need a hair of the dog,' he said. 'I need the whole coat.'

The wild cat jumped on his lap and sent him tumbling backwards on to the floor.

'Now, isn't that amazing,' said Hamish. 'Sonsie likes you.' He helped Jimmy back into his chair.

'If that's the result of liking, I'll settle for loathing any day. I hope Elspeth can get something.'

Elspeth was sitting in the Currie sisters' parlour, drinking tea. 'You should get that big loon to marry you,' said Nessie.

'Marry you,' muttered her sister, her eyes glued to the television set, watching a rerun of a Jerry Springer show.

Elspeth ignored that remark. 'I'd be interested to learn anything at all you know about Ina Braid.'

'Well, there's not much,' said Nessie. The

Greek chorus that was her sister was now thankfully immersed in the TV programme. 'Have a biscuit. I baked them yesterday.'

Elspeth dutifully bit into a buttery biscuit and waited. The wind yelled and shrieked along the waterfront as if all the demons of hell had been let loose.

Jessie wrinkled up her brow in thought. A downdraught blew peat smoke around the room but neither of the sisters seemed to notice. 'There's not much to tell,' said Nessie. 'Decent body and her sponge cake was as light as light. Not much to look at if you'd seen her afore she died but she was right pretty once. My, what a grand tennis player she was. Champion. Won the cup at the local championships over at Braikie. They had grand courts there but a building developer got his greedy hands on them and they're now houses where the courts were. My, that Ellie Macpherson, her what runs the post office in Braikie, was as mad as mad. Until Ina turned up, Ellie had been reigning champion.'

'Did they see much of each other?'

'No. Ellie was always a one to bear grudges.'

'Did Ina always get on all right with her husband?'

'Model couple, that's what they were.'

Elspeth persevered, but it seemed as if Ina had led a blameless life.

She decided to drive to Braikie and see Ellie. Elspeth left her photographer at the hotel. He was a tedious man, and she wanted as little of his company as possible.

But first, bending against the wind and carrying her laptop, she went into the *Highland Times* office and asked the editor, Matthew Campbell, if she could borrow a desk to send over some copy.

'Sure,' said Matthew, who had once worked alongside Elspeth in Glasgow before he had fallen in love with the local schoolteacher and decided to settle in the Highlands. 'Got anything interesting?'

'Not yet. Just a colour piece. You know, the hills and heather and blah, blah.'

'Take that desk over there.'

Elspeth switched on her computer and began to work. Hamish is going to hate me for this, she thought as she typed: 'Does a serial killer stalk the mountains and glens of the Highlands?'

When she had finished and was about to leave, Matthew said, 'Look, you could do me a favour. I've been getting our Angus to do the horoscopes, but he's down with the cold. Could you just bash out something? You used to do them when you worked here.'

'Oh, all right.'

Elspeth had an idea and began to type busily. For each star sign, she put in a veiled warning, slightly changed in each one. For Gemini, she wrote, 'Your sins will find you out. You were seen and whoever saw you is soon going to talk. You will have a sharp pain in your side on Thursday. Do not overwork and curb your volatile nature and propensity to indulge in violent rages.'

The others were all variations on the same theme.

She printed it off and handed it to Malcolm. He read it with his eyebrows raised. 'I'd better put a name other than Angus's at the top of this or someone might murder him, too. Suggest something?'

'Gypsy Rose?'

'Without the Lee? Okay.'

When Elspeth went out on to the waterfront to walk to her car, leaning against the force of the wind, it looked as if the whole countryside were in motion. Whitecapped waves scudded along the loch, clouds streamed across the sky, hedges in gardens sent out a mournful bagpipe sound as the wind whistled through them, and gates swung and banged on their hinges.

She hoped her small Mini Cooper was low enough on the road not to get blown over.

Fortunately the tide was out so that she was able to drive along the shore road into Braikie.

The bungalows that overlooked the road were now closed and falling into disrepair. They had been flooded so many times, the owners had been unable to sell them.

The whole coastline of Britain is being eaten away, thought Elspeth, and yet no one does anything about it.

She parked in the main street and went to the post office, which was closed for the half day. Elspeth remembered there was a flat above the post office. There was a door at the side with intercom. She pressed the bell. A high fluting voice demanded, 'Yees?'

'My name is Elspeth Grant. I'm from the *Daily Bugle*.' The door buzzed. Elspeth opened it and climbed up shallow stone steps to where a thin woman wearing a turban and with bare arms covered in bracelets stood waiting.

She struck a pose in the doorway and said, 'I see you have come to consult the Oracle.'

'The Oracle?'

'I know everything about everybody.'

'Well, that's good,' said Elspeth, following her in.

Incense was burning in the living room. A sofa and two armchairs were draped in violently coloured material, all red and yellow swirls. The carpet and walls were bright yellow. A bowl of yellow silk flowers stood on a round table by the window. Beside the bowl was a large crystal ball. A mobile of various crystal shapes hung from the ceiling. A bookshelf was crammed with books on astrology and the occult.

'Sherry?' offered Ellie.

'Yes, please. I didn't think anyone drank sherry any more.'

'My father, God rest his soul, always said that sherry was the only suitable drink for a lady.'

Ellie disappeared and returned with a tray with a decanter on it. But instead of sherry glasses, she poured the drink into two whisky tumblers.

'Slainte,' she said.

'Slainte,' echoed Elspeth. The sherry was heavy and sweet and had a faint chemical taste.

'Now sit down and tell me how I can help you.'

Elspeth sat down in one of the armchairs. Ellie put a little side table next to her covered with a lace doily.

'First question,' said Elspeth. 'Did you ever meet Catriona Beldame?'

'Yes. I suppose you heard that.'

Elspeth hadn't but maintained a discreet silence.

'I wanted to see if she was genuine,' said Ellie. 'There are so few of us about.'

'So few of what?'

'White witches.'

'Go on.'

'I did not stay long. I got out of that cottage as fast as I could.'

'Why?'

Ellie lowered her voice dramatically. 'She was a *black* witch. I can still hear her dreadful laughter as I ran away.'

Elspeth translated this as – I said something silly and she began to laugh and I was offended.

'I said to her as I fled, "The flames of hell will engulf you"' – Ellie leaned forward – 'and they did! I didn't put a curse on her, mind. That is not my way.'

This woman is bonkers, thought Elspeth. 'Do you know of anyone who might want to murder her?'

'It was the devil, come to claim his own.'

'And what about poor Ina Braid?'

A variety of emotions crossed Ellie's face. It was obvious she was trying desperately to think of something but that she didn't really know anything. 'There are things I could tell you,' she said.

'Then go on, do,' said Elspeth sharply. 'You are said to bear a grudge against Ina because she used to beat you at tennis.'

'That's because I let her win although I was always the better player. *I am a Christian*. I do not bear grudges.'

'Then who else might have disliked Ina?'

'I cannot. I would be putting my life in danger.'

Elspeth closed her notebook and got to her feet. 'Thank you for your time, Miss Macpherson. Got to rush.'

'Oh, do stay. There are other things I could tell you.'

But Elspeth was already out of the door and clattering down the steps.

Ellie was offended and felt thwarted as well. She had dreamt of featuring in the newspapers. When she opened up the post office for business the next day, she began to regale the customers with mysterious hints of how she really knew the identity of the murderer but was too afraid to say anything. The gossip swirled out from Braikie as if borne on the gale and spread around the surrounding villages.

Angela Brodie called on Hamish that evening.

'Come in,' he cried. 'I'm right weary. All I seem to do is question folk over and over again without getting anywhere.'

'Have you heard about Ellie Macpherson?'

'The postmistress?'

'Yes, her. Aren't you supposed to say post-person or something? I can't keep up with all this PC rubbish.'

'Don't ask me. I don't pay any attention to it. What about her?'

'Your friend Elspeth called on her. The Currie sisters told her that Ellie was a good fund of gossip. Now Ellie is saying that she knows the identity of the murderer but couldn't say anything because she fears for her life.'

'That's an awfully dangerous thing to say.'

'Don't worry about it. Ellie is a drama queen. Nobody takes her seriously.'

'A frightened murderer just might. Angela, have you heard anything, the slightest thing?'

'I'm afraid not, Hamish. And yet – I'm probably being overimaginative but it's as if there's a sort of communal secret in this village. I talk to people and I always get the feeling they are holding something back. You don't think the villagers would shield one of their own?'

'No, they would not. This business about Ellie bothers me. I'll take a run over to Braikie in the morning and tell the silly woman to keep her mouth shut.'

The gale was still blowing the next morning. Hamish fed his sheep and hens, told Sonsie and Lugs to look after themselves, and set off for Braikie. The incoming tide was threatening the shore road. He realized he would need to stay in Braikie until low tide came round again. It was possible to get into the town from two other roads, but that would have meant a long detour coming in from Lochdubh.

There was a small crowd standing outside the post office. 'What's happened to Ellie?' asked Hamish sharply.

'We don't know,' said one woman. 'She hasn't opened up and she hasn't answered her door.'

Hamish rang the bell himself. No reply. There was a narrow lane up the side of the post office. He went along it and around to the back of the building. He looked up at the window of Ellie's flat. It was not very high up. He hauled a dustbin up to the wall and climbed up on it. Then he grabbed the drainpipe and shinned up it so that he could look in at the window.

A sofa partially blocked his view but with a sinking heart he saw two feet protruding from the end of it.

Praying that she might just be ill, he clambered down and rushed round the front to his Land Rover, where he took out a police battering ram. A warning voice was telling him that he should phone Strathbane for permission before breaking in but he decided that losing time might mean he could not save Ellie's life.

'Keep back!' he ordered the crowd. He swung the battering ram with all his might and the door smashed open. He ran up the stairs. He tried her flat door and found it unlocked.

He went in.

Ellie was lying facedown on the carpet. The back of her head was a mess of blood. A crystal ball, smeared with blood, lay on the floor beside her. Hamish knelt down and felt for a pulse but there was no sign of life.

As he phoned Strathbane and slowly left the flat to stand guard outside, ignoring the babble of questions that greeted him, he felt a purely selfish pang of fear. There were now four murders, four *unsolved* murders. He knew that Blair, in order to turn attention away from himself, would say that he, Hamish, was incompetent and there was simply no reason to keep a police station in Lochdubh when Strathbane had to come over and do all the work.

He waited a long time. He realized they had probably tried to take the shore road, found their way blocked by the tide, and had to circle around to reach the upper road.

The crowd grew larger by the minute but now they stood in silence.

At last he heard the approaching sirens. The procession was headed by the procurator fiscal's BMW, an unmarked police car followed by two police vans, the forensic van, the pathologist's car, a fire engine and an ambulance.

The procurator fiscal, Mr Ian Bell-Sinclair, was Hamish's least favourite person next to Blair. He was fat, pompous and lazy. The job of the procurator fiscal in Scotland is broadly the same as that of a coroner in other legal systems. He is also supposed to direct police investigations and take statements from witnesses. Unless any of the press were around, Bell-Sinclair shirked as many of his duties as possible.

He ignored Hamish and turned to Jimmy and his sidekick, Andy MacNab. 'Where is your boss?'

'The detective chief inspector is not very well this morning,' said Jimmy. He turned to Hamish. 'Let's have it.'

Hamish flatly described what he had found. 'I hope you applied for permission before breaking in,' said the procurator fiscal.

'And he got it,' said Jimmy impatiently. 'Let's go in. Suit up, Hamish.'

Hamish went to the Land Rover, got out his forensic suit and put it on. He went back and led Jimmy up to the flat. Bell-Sinclair retreated to his car. He was famous for his detestation of viewing dead bodies.

'Why her?' asked Jimmy.

Hamish told him about Angela's visit and how he had learned that Ellie had been bragging that she knew the murderer.

'Think she did?'

'I don't know. I'll go out and phone Elspeth. She interviewed her the other day.'

Hamish went back outside and sat in the Land Rover. He was just about to phone Elspeth when he saw her with a photographer on the other side of one of the barriers the police had used to block off the street.

He got out and went up to her, saying to the policeman at the barricade, 'Let her through. She's a witness. No, not the photographer, Elspeth. Just you.'

'She's dead, isn't she?' said Elspeth.

'Let's go to my vehicle. I need a statement from you.'

Elspeth described her interview with Ellie and ended by saying, 'I'll swear she was just showing off. If Ellie knew the identity of the murderer, she would have told the police and then phoned all the newspapers. But someone got to hear of it and took her seriously.'

'Let's hope you're wrong and Jimmy finds some evidence of something. I almost hope this murder has got nothing to do with the others.'

'Is that all? I've got to file a story.'

'Yes, for now. Call on me later.'

'Will do. Jimmy's just come out and your girlfriend's just gone in.'

'Lesley is not my girlfriend.'

'If you say so.'

Hamish saw Elspeth stop by the procurator fiscal's car. Bell-Sinclair got out, and they exchanged a few words. Then they walked towards the police barrier. Bell-Sinclair struck a pose and Elspeth's photographer took a picture of him.

How that man does love his photo in the press, thought Hamish. He went to join Jimmy and told him what Elspeth had said.

'Well, Hamish, it's the usual old drudgery. We can't tell yet when she was killed. Get into that crowd and the shops around and ask if anyone saw anything.'

Hamish spent a weary day, asking question after question. Of course, there were always a few imaginative people who would swear they saw a sinister figure lurking around, but further questioning and an invitation to the police station for an interview always had them backtracking like mad.

By the end of the day, he began to wonder why he went on punishing himself by remaining a common bobby. If he had upgraded to detective, then he would be in the middle of knowing everything that was going on with the investigation. On the other hand, that would mean moving to Strathbane, working at first on the beat and then sitting and passing the necessary exams. He would need to move into police accommodation, and that would mean getting rid of Sonsie and Lugs. He consoled himself with the thought that Jimmy usually kept him well informed.

Hard on that thought came the other worry. Four murders and not a clue! He hadn't bothered to ask what ailed Blair, assuming it to be one of his usual alcoholic troubles, but even from his sickbed Blair was, he knew, capable of putting the boot in, yammering on about how incompetent Hamish had turned out to be.

As he wearily returned to his Land Rover, all around the press were having a field day. Television vans were lined up outside the police barriers. The voices of TV reporters talking about 'the highland serial killer' were blown towards him on the decreasing wind.

He drove back to the police station and fed his pets. He felt too tired to feed himself. He almost wished Lesley would arrive carrying her stew pot.

He went into the office, typed up his report, and sent it off. That finished, he decided to treat himself to a meal.

Hamish went out on to the waterfront. The wind had died down but angry waves still rose and fell on the loch, crashing down on the shingle of the shore and retreating with a hissing sound.

Willie Lamont welcomed him and gave him a table by the window. Hamish ordered a dish of lasagne and half a bottle of wine.

When Willie arrived with the wine, Hamish said, 'You've heard about the murder of Ellie?'

'Aye. Bad business. Evidently herself was bragging about how she knew who the murderer was. She even wrote up the horoscopes for the paper, practically saying she knew who it was.'

'Are you sure she wrote the horoscopes? Have you got the paper?'

'Just out today. I've got a copy in the kitchen. I'll get it for you.'

When he returned with the paper, Hamish read the horoscopes. His heart sank. He was sure it was Elspeth's work and nothing to do with Ellie. He took out his phone and called Matthew Campbell.

'Yes, it was Elspeth,' said Matthew. 'Angus usually does them but he's ill and I asked Elspeth to do them in return for the use of a desk in the office.'

Hamish felt a pang of fear. How stupid of Elspeth. 'Don't dare tell anyone at all who wrote them,' he said.

'They'll think it was Angus.'

'So that puts his life at risk. Damn, I'd better get up there.'

When his food arrived, Hamish gulped it down, paid his bill, and set off up the hill to the seer's cottage.

To his relief, Angus himself answered the door.

'Can I come in?' asked Hamish. 'I've come to warn you.'

'I'm fine now, Hamish. What's it about? I know. I've seen the paper. They'll think it was me. Who was it?'

'Never mind. Have you a spare bed, Angus?'

'Just the one.'

'I'll go back and get my sleeping bag. I'm staying here tonight.'

Hamish returned half an hour later, followed by Sonsie and Lugs. 'I'm off to bed,' said Angus. 'I've kept the fire lit for you.'

Hamish had changed into civilian clothes. He crawled into his sleeping bag, fully dressed. He even left his boots on.

The floor was hard but he was so tired he immediately fell asleep. During the night a long low hiss awakened him. He opened his eyes, feeling the weight of his wild cat on his chest. In the light of the fire, Sonsie's yellow eyes burned red and her fur was standing up on her back.

'Good girl,' whispered Hamish, shoving her off. He eased himself out of the sleeping bag and then sat up and listened.

All was silent – and then he heard a faint rustling sound from outside. He rose up, went to the door, and opened it. The brae stretched out empty in the moonlight. 'Who's there?' he called.

Silence.

He walked around the cottage but could see no one.

In the morning, he said to Angus, 'Is there any place you could go for a few days? I've a feeling there was someone after you last night.'

'I could go to my friend in Ardgay. He'll aye put me up.'

'Do that, Angus. How did you know about Fiona McNulty?'

'My psychic powers.'

'Havers. Someone told you. I wish you really had psychic powers and you could tell me the identity of this murderer.'

'It will come to me. My cold blocked out the spirit world.'

'Och, just get packed and get off,' said Hamish.

After Angus had left in his battered old van, Hamish went back to the police station, showered and changed into his uniform, settled his pets and told them they were on their own for the day, and then phoned Jimmy. He told him his fears about Angus, caused by Elspeth doing the horoscopes.

'Is she stupid or something?' said Jimmy. 'If our murderer learns it was her and not Angus, she'll be the next on the dead list. We haven't the manpower to guard her. Go and tell her from me to get back to Glasgow.'

Hamish drove up to the Tommel Castle Hotel and asked Mr Johnson if he knew where Elspeth was.

'All the press were off early and over to Braikie,' said the manager. 'Try there.'

'Try her room first,' urged Hamish. 'She may have stayed behind to work on an article.'

The manager phoned. Elspeth answered, and hearing it was Hamish who was looking for her, said she would come downstairs.

Elspeth was wearing a ratty old sweater over faded jeans and large clumpy boots. Hamish wished she'd dress up a bit, put on a skirt, and then wondered whether, if he ever married, he would turn into the sort of bullying husband who chose his wife's clothes.

'You look anxious,' said Elspeth. 'What's up?'

'Let's go through to the lounge and find a quiet corner. This is serious.'

When they were seated, Hamish leaned forward and said, 'Elspeth, you wrote those horoscopes in the *Highland Times*.'

'Yes, Matthew was stuck because Ang—'

'I know. I had to sleep at Angus's place last night.'

'Why? Is he still ill?' Her eyes widened. 'You think the murderer thinks it was him and might come after him?'

'Yes, I think someone tried to get him last

night. Now, if it leaks out it was you, you'll be at risk. I want you to go back to Glasgow.'

'I can't, Hamish. This is big stuff. Four murders! The news desk will ask me why I want to leave the scene and if I say I've been writing for another paper, they'll sack me.'

'Can I get you anything?'

Both looked up, startled. One of the Polish waitresses, a tall girl with red hair, was looming over them. Hamish remembered her name was Anya Kowalski.

'No, Anya,' said Hamish.

When she went away, Hamish said, 'I wonder how long she was standing there.'

'I think my radar is out of kilter,' said Elspeth. 'I don't know. But I am not going to quit this story, Hamish. I can look after myself.'

Anxiety made Hamish's temper flare. 'You're a silly wee girl!'

'Don't you dare patronize me. If you're so worried about me, get off your arse and go and find out who is doing this.' Elspeth got to her feet. 'If you concentrated as hard on looking for a murderer as you do looking after those pets of yours, you might get somewhere.'

Hamish stood up and smiled maliciously. 'Dear me, lassie. I never thought the day would come when you'd be jealous o' a couple o' beasties.'

Elspeth turned on her heel and strode off.

Hamish sat down again and phoned Jimmy. 'She won't leave,' he said.

'I put in a report about it after you called,' said Jimmy. 'The procurator fiscal says that as we've enough Strathbane men on the ground asking questions, you're to guard Elspeth yourself. He's got a soft spot for her because a flattering picture of him and comment appeared in the *Bugle* today.'

'We had a row,' said Hamish. 'How can I guard her when she won't speak to me?'

'Ah, love,' said Jimmy. 'Make it up and keep after her.'

Hamish left the lounge just as Elspeth was descending the stairs with her coat on. She had completed her ensemble by putting on one of those mushroom-shaped Afghan hats.

'I'm sorry if I upset you, Elspeth,' said Hamish quickly. 'I've got an idea. Why don't we join forces for the day?'

She looked up at him. 'Been ordered to guard me?'

'I see your radar's working again. What I really want to do is get down to Perth and interview Ruby Connachie. I want to start at the beginning. I want to find out as much about Catriona as possible. There's someone in her background somewhere that started all this off.'

'Hamish, the murderer might be right here in Lochdubh.'

'Then there's a chance that someone in the village might have known Catriona before she ever came up here.'

'Right you are. I could do with some colour for a background piece.'

'Off we go, then. Let's start all over again with the first murder.'

Chapter Eight

Thou tyrant, tyrant Jealousy,
Thou tyrant of the mind!
– John Dryden

Hamish first went to the police station and got Ruby Connachie's address from the computer.

Jimmy stepped out in front of the mobile police unit and held up a hand to stop Hamish as he was driving off.

'Where are you going?' he demanded.

'Here, there and anywhere,' said Hamish, waving a vague hand. 'I have to protect Elspeth here and so I'm taking her right out of the village for the day.'

'Okay, off you go, but remember the lassie's a journalist and don't be talking off the record.'

'As if I would,' said Hamish piously.

Much as he desperately wanted to solve the murders, Hamish had a guilty feeling of holiday as he drove off. It was like old times to be with Elspeth again. What did she think of him these days? Should he marry her? It would be grand to be married and maybe have a couple of children.

'You've got a silly smile on your face,' said Elspeth. 'What are you thinking about?'

'The scenery,' lied Hamish. 'It's a grand day.'

'It is indeed,' said Elspeth as they sped up over the heathery hills.

That remark about his silly smile had irked Hamish. The dream of marriage to Elspeth disappeared and he began to wonder if Ruby could actually give them any leads.

Known to the Romans as Bertha from the Celtic Aber The, meaning 'the mouth of the River Tay', Perth has been a Royal Burgh since the thirteenth century and was a royal residence through the middle ages. With its parks and Georgian houses, it is still one of the fairest of Scotland's cities.

But like all towns and cities in Scotland, it had its housing estates, and it was in one of these that Ruby Connachie lived.

'She must be pretty old by now,' said Elspeth.

'From the reports, I gather she's seventy-six and got all her marbles – well, those that haven't been cracked by jealousy.'

'So she was jealous of Catriona?'

'Seems that way. She says Burrell doted on

the girl for all he was strict. Here we are. I don't suppose any of the local police will be visiting her again, so with luck Jimmy will never find out where we have been.'

Ruby lived in a block of 'sheltered' housing for the elderly on the estate. Her flat was on the first floor.

Hamish rang the doorbell. There was a long silence.

'I hope the woman's alive,' whispered Hamish.

'I sense someone in there,' said Elspeth.

After what seemed an age there was a sound of shuffling feet on the other side of the door. Then it creaked open on a chain.

A small, wrinkled face peered up at Hamish. 'Who are you?'

Hamish introduced himself but not Elspeth in the hope that she would think Elspeth was a plainclothes policewoman. The door shut, and then came the sound of elderly fingers struggling to undo the chain. The door swung open again, revealing Ruby to be a small, old woman leaning on a Zimmer frame. Her figure was stooped and her grey hair, thin and sparse, showed patches of pink scalp.

The door opened directly into a small living room. It was simply furnished with two easy chairs, two hard-backed chairs, a small television set, and two occasional tables, one of which held a framed photograph of a younger Ruby on the arm of a heavyset man.

Hamish picked it up. 'Is this Mr Burrell?'

'Yes, that's him. We would have been married if that fiend hadn't murdered him. He put it off too long. "As soon as Catriona goes to university, we'll get married," he'd say.'

'What was Catriona like?'

'Sleekit. That's what she was. Sleekit. You would think butter wouldn't melt in her mouth. Yes, Daddy. No, Daddy. When she said she was at the library, studying, I told him I saw her hanging out in the High Street with a group of boys. When he challenged her, she burst into tears and said, "I was only talking to a group of school friends." And he believed her! I knew if I told any more tales on her, the wedding would be off.'

'Do you think anyone from the time she lived in Perth would want to kill her?'

Ruby gave an asthmatic chuckle. 'Apart from me? I mind there was this young fellow, Wayne Abercrombie. I was visiting my Horace . . .'

'Horace being Mr Burrell?' asked Hamish.

'Yes. This lad Wayne came hammering at the door demanding to speak to Catriona. Horace said she was out. Wayne said he had to see her to find out whether she meant to go through with the abortion. I thought poor Horace was going to drop dead with a heart attack. He told him to get lost or he'd call the police and he sent me home and waited for Catriona. I phoned him the next day and he wouldn't speak about it except to say that it was all lies and he didn't want to hear about it again.

'Oh, I wanted proof. I wanted something against her to open his eyes to what she was really like. I went in search of Wayne. He was older than Catriona and working at a garage out on the Inverness Road. Well, he tried to deny even having been at the house! Then he said it had all been a joke.'

'Where is he now?'

'He married a local lass a whiles back. I remember seeing the wedding in the local paper. He was a motor mechanic so maybe he's in the same job. I always wonder if he was the one that stole the money.'

'What money?' asked Elspeth.

'It was the night of the day that Wayne had come to the house. Someone broke in during the night and stole five hundred pounds that Horace had in his desk. He kept it to pay workmen off the books. I know it sounds bad that a churchman should pay workers off the books but a lot of them, because of the VAT and the health and safety regulations, won't work unless it's for cash. The police were called. The lock on the front door had been jemmied open. Horace couldn't understand why he didn't wake because he was aye a light sleeper. You know what I think? I think that bitch from hell gave him some sort of sleeping pill and stole the money herself.'

'Did you tell the police any of this?' asked Hamish. 'I don't remember anything in the report.'

'No, it was a young female detective wi' a snippy way about her. I don't think she wanted to bother listening to me.'

After they had left her, Hamish said they should start asking at all the garages they could find and see if they could trace Wayne Abercrombie.

They were lucky first time. He was still working at the garage out on the Inverness Road.

He was a tall man with a thick thatch of brown hair and a pleasant tanned face. But on hearing that they wanted to ask him about Catriona, he scowled and said it was all in the past and he had to get on with his work. Only Hamish's threat to take him down to the police station made him sigh and say, 'Let's get out of here. I'll tell them I'm taking a break and it's about a stolen car.'

He came back shortly and stripped off his oily overalls. 'Let's go over to the pub,' he said.

Over a pint of beer, he reluctantly began his story. 'Catriona was a wild one. I swear to God she seduced me. I mean, she was still a schoolgirl and her father a minister, but she got me fair worked up. Then she told me she was pregnant and I would have to marry her. I didn't want to. There was something about her that frightened me. But I thought I'd better do the decent thing and call on her and see her father as well because she said if I didn't marry her she would get an abortion. He wouldn't believe me and said he'd call the police.

'The next day, Catriona turns up here and hands me five hundred pounds and tells me to keep my mouth shut and that never to tell anyone we had had sex. I asked about the baby. She sneered and said there wasn't any baby. She just wanted to get married and get out of that house.'

'When did you last see her?' asked Hamish.

He hung his head.

'Out with it?' said Hamish sharply.

'A chap came in for repairs, a tourist, and we got to talking. He was an Australian. He said the villages were fascinating and one even had a resident witch. Her name was Catriona Beldame and he had a photo of her. I suddenly wanted to see her. I wanted to know if perhaps she really had been pregnant and had our child. So I went up there.'

'When?' demanded Hamish sharply.

'It must have been the week afore she was murdered. She was very bitter.'

'In what way?'

'She blamed everyone, starting with her father. Then she blamed me for seducing a schoolgirl. I pointed out she had seduced me and that's when she got furious and started screaming at me to get out. That's all. I swear I had nothing to do with her murder.'

Hamish took him through the other three murders but he had cast-iron alibis for all of them.

'Will this need to come out?' he asked. 'I don't want the wife to know.'

'I'll try to keep it quiet,' said Hamish.

'So what do you think of what we've got so far?' asked Elspeth over lunch.

'Not much,' said Hamish gloomily. 'I had great hopes of Wayne.'

'Might be him after all.'

'I'm sure not. I don't want to alert Jimmy to the fact that I'm in Perth where he told me not to go.'

'That Niçoise salad of yours is going to wilt if you don't eat it, Hamish.'

'I keep thinking I ought to eat more healthy food and yet when I get it, my appetite goes away.'

'I can put you on my expenses. Send it back and order a steak.'

'It's a waste.'

'I'm only having salad, so I can eat two.' Elspeth called over the waiter and ordered Hamish a T-bone steak and chips.

'If only Catriona had been a nice person like Ina Braid. So many people must have wanted to murder her,' mourned Hamish.

'Now, there's a thing. What about Ina Braid? Surely the only reason she was murdered was because she knew something. She must have said something to her husband. Let's go back and see him.'

'I've just remembered,' said Hamish. 'Ina's funeral is this afternoon. I'll ask for a doggy bag and take the steak with me. We've got to be there.'

'It's only on the TV that murderers turn up at funerals, Hamish.'

'I'd still like to be there.'

When they arrived, the church service was over and everyone was at the graveside. The whole village had turned out.

'Are you coming to the village hall afterwards?' asked Angela, appearing beside them. 'The women decided that Fergus couldn't cope with the entertaining and so they're organizing the funeral baked meats for him.'

'We'll take a look in. I'd better contribute some whisky if Patel has any left. How's Fergus coping?'

'He's pretty shattered. It all seems to have finally hit him hard.'

When the graveside ceremony was over, Elspeth and Hamish bought a bottle of whisky and followed the black-clad figures to the hall. At other funerals, people might now turn up in colours, but Lochdubh kept to the tradition of funereal black.

At the hall, Tilly Framont came up to Hamish, her eyes wet with tears. 'I've lost my best friend,' she said.

'Did Ina not tell you something about the murder of Catriona?' asked Hamish.

'No, all she said was "good riddance". And she wasn't a secretive woman.'

Tilly moved away.

Nessie Currie then approached them. Jessie was over at the buffet, loading up a plate with sandwiches.

She glared at Elspeth. 'Thon was a really stupid set of horoscopes,' she said.

Was it Hamish's imagination, or was there not a sudden silence all around? People were still talking but he had an uneasy feeling that someone close by had been shocked by what Nessie had said.

'Sorry about that,' said Elspeth, 'but Angus was off sick and I did the best I could.'

'You should be ashamed of yourself, meddling with people's star signs. I'm a Scorpio.'

'You are that,' said Hamish and led Elspeth off to the buffet.

'How long is this guard of yours to go on?' asked Elspeth.

'I'll try to look after you for as long as possible, but for my sake and your own, try to get off to Glasgow soon.'

A splash of colour appeared in the doorway of the hall. 'Oh, look, it's your girlfriend,' said Elspeth. 'I'm off to circulate. I'll have to report on this. I see my photographer's got a glass in his hand. I'd better find out whether he got some decent pictures before he gets too drunk.'

Lesley, wearing a cherry-red coat, joined Hamish. 'What are you doing here?' asked Hamish.

'I came to see you. I thought you might like to know the latest developments.'

'There are a couple of empty chairs over in the corner,' said Hamish. 'Let's go over there.'

'I went back over the mobile home myself,' said Lesley, 'and I found one thread – a dark blue thread, which might have come off a tweed coat or jacket. It was a lucky find because whoever murdered Fiona vacuumed up afterwards and took away the vacuum bag. I thought you might want to look around for someone with a jacket or coat like that.'

'Thanks. That's a good tip,' said Hamish, thinking Lesley looked pretty with her large eyes and red-gold hair.

'I couldn't find you today,' said Lesley. 'Where were you?'

'I've been babysitting my reporter friend. She wrote the horoscope article in the local paper implying she knew the identity of the murderer.'

'That's odd.'

'What is?'

'Getting you to babysit. That should be a job for a policewoman.'

'Elspeth has helped out on cases in the past. I think Jimmy hoped she would come up with something. Oh, here's the lord and master.'

Blair pushed his way through the throng. 'I've just learned you've been wasting your time squiring around your girlfriend. I gave Anderson a rocket. These journalists are hard-boiled and don't need protection. Get up to Braikie and start asking folks all over again. Someone must ha' seen something.'

'I'll tell her,' said Hamish.

Blair saw the trays of whisky being carried around, and his eyes gleamed. 'No, laddie, I'll tell her. Get off with you.'

Lesley walked out with him. 'Maybe you'll be free for dinner tonight?' said Hamish. 'I owe you one.'

'I would like that.'

'The Italian place at eight?'

'Fine.'

* * *

Hamish felt the rest of the day was a waste of time. No one in Braikie had seen anything. Even the ones who said they had, the ones who had made up colourful stories, had nothing now to say.

When he got to the restaurant that evening, Lesley was the only customer. From the village hall came the sound of the accordion and fiddle. The wake would go on all night as usual, he guessed.

Lesley was wearing a low-cut blue dress revealing a deep cleavage. Hamish felt the first stirrings of desire. Elspeth had been cool and business-like and had put out no vibes at all. Her very style of dress seemed to say *keep off*.

Lesley found Hamish more attractive than ever. The fact that here was a man who didn't seem to want to drag her off to bed had piqued her curiosity about him, and his friendship with Elspeth had roused her competitive instincts.

They talked over the murder cases and drank quite a lot of wine. Hamish, just before the coffee was served, reached across the table and took her hand.

'Lesley,' he began, when a familiar voice said, 'Gosh I'm beat. Am I in time for coffee?'

Elspeth pulled up a chair and sat down. Hamish drew back his hand as if he had been scalded.

'Find out anything?' he asked.

'Nothing. But I've arranged I should call on Fergus tomorrow.'

'You shouldnae have done that without checking with me first.'

Elspeth looked from Hamish to Lesley. 'Dear me, it seems as if I am not welcome here.'

'Who's not welcome?' said a cool, amused voice.

Hamish stumbled to his feet, his face flaming. 'Priscilla! When did you arrive?'

'Today. May I join you? Hello, Elspeth. Who's this?'

Hamish introduced Priscilla to Lesley, aware the whole time of the malicious amusement in Elspeth's silver eyes.

Lesley's heart sank. Who on earth was this classy vision, impeccably dressed, serene and beautiful? Her face was perfect, as was the smooth bell of her blonde hair. Lesley had drunk a lot so that she would have the excuse of asking Hamish for a bed for the night. It was still worth a try.

'I'm afraid I'm not in a fit condition to drive this evening,' she said.

'Don't worry about it,' said Priscilla. 'I'll put you up at the hotel as my guest.'

All Lesley could do was to say dismally, 'Very kind of you.'

Priscilla wanted to know all about the murders.

Lesley felt forgotten as Hamish described all the murders and Priscilla listened intently.

'Look,' she interrupted at last, 'I really think I'm fit to drive home.'

'How rude of me to ignore you like this,' said Priscilla. 'Hamish, I'll catch up with you tomorrow.'

When they had gone Elspeth asked, 'Feeling smug?'

'No. Why?'

'Our forensic expert is after you.'

Hamish looked uncomfortable. 'I think maybe she's just keen on her job. Look, I'll come with you to see Fergus. Has anyone come forward to claim Catriona's body for burial?'

'Not that I've heard. I believe Mrs Wellington was trying to get the villagers to raise money for her funeral but the general opinion is that a stake through the heart is all that's needed. But I suppose the responsibility will fall on the husband.'

'I gather Fergus is still off work?'

'He's thinking of going back soon.'

'I forgot to ask Jimmy whether Ina was insured.'

'We'll ask tomorrow.'

Hamish sighed. 'I'd better escort you to the hotel. Remember to lock your door and don't answer without checking downstairs first.'

* * *

Fergus answered the door to them the following morning. He looked a wreck. His eyes were bloodshot and his shoulders stooped. 'Come ben,' he said.

What had happened to Ina's impeccable housekeeping? Empty beer cans lay on the floor along with the remains of TV dinners. The furniture was covered in a thin layer of dust.

'You're not looking very well,' commented Hamish.

'Ina looked after me real well. I can't cook. I hate shopping. Och, man, I wish she was back.' Fergus began to cry.

'Wheesht, now,' said Hamish. 'You'll just need to get used to the fact that she's gone.'

'I'll make a cup of tea,' said Elspeth, and she disappeared into the kitchen.

'Are you all right financially?' asked Hamish.

'Oh, aye.' Fergus gave a great gulping sob and wiped his nose on his sleeve. 'Her life was insured.'

'How much?'

'Seventy-five thousand pounds. Thon creature Blair was trying to make me admit I murdered her for the money but he can't prove otherwise.'

'Maybe you should take a holiday,' said Elspeth. 'Get right away.'

'I can't. Hamish, you've just got to find out who killed my Ina.'

'Fergus, I think she knew something about the killer,' said Hamish. 'Didn't she even give you a hint about who it might be?'

'No, but we didnae talk all that much come to think of it. I watched the telly of an evening and herself would knit or go out to one of those women's meetings at the kirk.'

'I want you to keep thinking about it all the same,' said Hamish earnestly. 'Anything at all she might have said.'

'Now what?' asked Elspeth when they were outside. The day was still and misty, and little pearls of moisture glinted in her frizzy hair.

'I think I'll get back ower to Bonar Bridge. Maybe I might pick up something there.'

'Want me to come with you?'

'No, just be careful.'

Hamish wanted rid of her because he wanted to see Priscilla. He wondered if the old longing for her would ever go away.

He returned to the police station to collect his dog and cat, making sure first that no members of the press were lurking about, and then drove to the hotel.

The Tommel Castle Hotel had once been the home of the Halburton-Smythes. It was one of those mock Gothic castles that had sprung up in the Highlands in Victoria's reign when landowners wanted to copy Balmoral. Colonel Halburton-Smythe had fallen on hard times, and it was Hamish who had suggested he turn his home into a hotel. The establishment had flourished, and the colonel was fond of bragging that it had all been his own idea.

He asked for Priscilla and was told she was over in the gift shop helping the new Polish girl with the stock. Hamish uneasily remembered talking to Elspeth in the lounge and looking up and seeing that Polish maid. Had she said anything about Elspeth writing the horoscopes? Then he reflected dismally that even if she hadn't, the gossip grapevine of Lochdubh had probably found out already. Nessie Currie would have seen to that.

He wondered if any of the villagers were protecting someone. He desperately didn't want it to be anyone from the village.

He opened the door of the gift shop and went in. Priscilla and a Polish girl were sorting out a box of Shetland wool shawls, all of them as fine as gossamer.

'I'm just about finished here,' said Priscilla. 'Want to talk?'

'Yes,' said Hamish. 'If you can spare the time.'

She smiled. 'I've always got time for you.'

Hamish turned away to hide the sudden rush of gladness on his face.

Priscilla finished giving the girl instructions and then said, 'Let's go. I could do with a coffee.'

Elspeth arrived to pick up her laptop just as they were both disappearing into the hotel. Straight back to her like a homing pigeon, thought Elspeth. He only said he was going to Bonar to get rid of me.

They sat in the lounge. Hamish could remember when it had been the family drawing room. Priscilla ordered coffee and biscuits and asked, 'How far have you got today?'

Hamish told her about the interview with Fergus. 'It might be an idea to go over and see this paper mill,' said Priscilla. 'It's just outside Strathbane on this side, isn't it?'

'Maybe I'll go there,' said Hamish. 'Although I feel I should really be keeping an eye on Elspeth.'

'Oh, the horoscopes.'

'How did you find out?'

'From the barman. I don't know where he got it from. But don't worry about Elspeth. She's a good reporter, and good reporters know how to take care of themselves. When we finish our coffee we'll go over.'

'We?'

'Yes, we.'

Hamish was driving them along the road to Strathbane when he suddenly said, 'There's a

Land Rover following us and I think I recognize it. I think it belongs to two deer poachers I arrested. They must be out on bail. We might be in for a bit of trouble.'

'Got your rifle?'

'In the back.'

Priscilla began to climb over into the back of the Land Rover. 'What are you doing?' cried Hamish.

'I'd feel better if we were armed. Where is the ammo? Oh, got it. Are they coming closer?'

'Yes, they must have a souped-up engine. I'll call for backup.'

He looked in the rearview mirror and saw a gun protruding from the passenger side of the pursuing vehicle. 'Get down, Priscilla,' he shouted.

He felt a blast of cold air as Priscilla lowered one of the windows in the back. 'Keep straight, Hamish. Don't swerve. I'm going to shoot their tyres out.'

There was a blast of gunfire and Priscilla cried, 'Got 'em. Stop, Hamish. They've gone off the road.'

'Stay where you are,' said Hamish, jumping out of the Land Rover, but Priscilla joined him, carrying the rifle.

Hamish phoned for backup. Then he said to Priscilla, 'They're armed. We're not going down there on our own.'

'How unexciting,' said Priscilla calmly. 'Can

you see where they've gone? It's hard to make out anything in this mist.'

The poachers' vehicle had gone off the edge of the road and down a steep heathery slope.

'No,' said Hamish. 'They must have gone down a good way. You're a good shot, Priscilla.'

'Haven't lost my touch,' she said.

'Are the dog and cat all right?'

'They seem to be. I'll let them out. Is there going to be a fuss about me being with you, Hamish?'

'No. I haven't had a day off in ages. I'll say it's my time off. Daviot's such a snob, he won't dare complain about you being with me.'

When an armed squad arrived headed by Daviot, Hamish waited patiently, thinking of all the paperwork he would have to do if the men had been killed in the crash or even injured.

Blair then arrived and was looking about to blast Hamish when he saw Daviot talking to Priscilla, and his face fell.

Hamish told him what had happened. 'Your day off, is it?' demanded Blair. 'And who gie'd ye the permission?'

'I did,' said Jimmy's voice behind Blair. 'Constable Macbeth hasn't had a day off in ages.'

The mist began to swirl and thin in a rising wind. The leader of the armed force came back up the brae. 'Their vehicle's there but they're long gone. Their Land Rover ran into a big rock right down at the bottom o' the hill. The thick heather must ha' slowed their speed, because there's hardly a dunt in the vehicle.'

'I want a full search for them,' ordered Daviot. 'Hamish, I will let you and Miss Halburton-Smythe get on, but I will expect a statement from you by this evening. Do give that rifle to Detective Anderson. If you shot one of the men by mistake, then we will need it for evidence.'

'I shot the tyre out,' said Priscilla. 'I never miss.' She laughed and held out the rifle to Jimmy. A flash went off. Hamish cursed. Elspeth and her photographer were standing at the edge of the group.

Elspeth came forward. 'I would appreciate a statement, Superintendent Daviot.'

Daviot forced a smile. Elspeth had always been kind to the police. 'Very well, Miss Grant.'

'Come along, Priscilla,' whispered Hamish urgently. 'Let's get out of here before Daviot sees the dog and cat. Neither of them has as good a pedigree as you, and Daviot will give me a bollocking for taking them around in a police vehicle.'

They drove off. When they were well clear of the scene, Priscilla said, 'Stop!'

'What is it? Are they back?'

'No, I feel a bit sick and shaky.'

'And here's me thinking you were made of iron. I'll take you back.'

'No, let's go on. I'll be all right in a minute.'

The manager of the paper works, Mr Benjamin Worthy, looked at them both impatiently when Hamish asked whether Fergus could possibly have left the works unnoticed.

'I've been through all this before,' he said. Worthy was one of those lowland Scots who should never be put in charge of anyone. He had a brusque, bullying manner. He was small and round, wearing a suit, collar and tie. He had small, black eyes in a discontented face.

'As I said already, they clock in here and clock out. There is only one way out of this factory for the men and that is past the security guard at the entrance.'

'But your trucks go in and out,' Hamish pointed out.

'Fergus Braid is not a truck driver. He is a machine operator.'

'Has he got any special friend here?'

'Is this necessary?'

'Oh, yes.'

'I'll get the foreman.'

He bustled out, leaving them in his pretentious office with its framed Rotary Club photographs on the walls and its oversize desk.

After what seemed like a long time to Hamish and Priscilla, the door opened and a man in blue overalls came in. 'I'm Mike Haggerty,' he said. 'The foreman. The boss said you had some questions.'

'Did Fergus Braid have any special friend at the works?'

'You could maybe say that was me. We often grabbed a drink after work.'

'Could Fergus possibly have left the works on the day of his wife's murder without anyone knowing?'

The foreman was tall and thin with thick glasses. A ray of sun shone in the window. The mist had lifted. Hamish noticed a thin film of sweat on Mike's brow.

Hamish's eyes sharpened. He decided to guess. 'I know you covered for him,' he said sternly. 'You may as well tell the truth or I'll haul you in and charge you with impeding the police in their inquiries.'

'He wouldnae hurt a fly, Fergus wouldn't.' blustered Mike. 'He only wanted a couple of hours so I told him he could nip out through the lorry bay at the back.'

'And why didn't you report this before?'

'Because there was one nasty swine o' a detective bullying me and more or less telling me that Fergus had murdered Ina, and Fergus would never do such a thing.'

'Wait there,' ordered Hamish. He nodded to

Priscilla, and they stepped outside. With a heavy heart, Hamish took out his phone and called Jimmy.

'Great!' enthused Jimmy, when Hamish had finished speaking. 'So he didn't have the day off and that water bailiff must have been lying. Keep an eye on the bugger. I'll be right over.'

When the foreman was taken away, Hamish sadly went back to the Land Rover with Priscilla and drove off. 'I only hope Fergus comes up with an alibi and a real one this time. I chust can't believe that man would murder his wife. Blair will try to pin the other murders on him as well.'

Chapter Nine

The cruellest lies are often told in silence.
– Robert Louis Stevenson

The arrest of Fergus Braid struck the village like a bombshell. Lesley, opening the newspaper the next day, found a photograph of him on the front page and a different story on the inside. HIGHLAND BOBBY ATTACKED BY ARMED POACHERS screamed the headline. There was a photograph of Priscilla laughing as she handed the rifle over. Lesley read the story carefully. There was nothing about why Priscilla was on the scene and why she had a rifle. She did not know Priscilla's involvement had been suppressed.

Lesley scowled. Priscilla was *real* competition. All Hamish needed was the support of a strong ambitious woman who could get him out of that village and into the mainstream of police work. For all his intelligence, she suspected he was shy.

She decided she would invite him to her flat in Strathbane for dinner. That way she would be safe from interruptions.

Elspeth received a call from the features editor. 'I'm sending up Perry Gaunt.'

'But I've done two colour features for you,' complained Elspeth.

'The editor wants to give Perry a break. Book him a room and show him the ropes. He'll be with you shortly. He set off yesterday. He was planning to spend an overnight in Inverness.'

Elspeth knew it was futile to protest further. Perry Gaunt was an old Etonian, and his father was a close friend of the London editor.

No sooner had she put down the phone in her room than it rang again. It was Mr Johnson. 'There's a Mr Gaunt asking for you.'

'I'll be right down,' said Elspeth.

Perry Gaunt was leaning on the reception desk. He was tall and lean with thick fair hair and a pleasant face. He was wearing an expensive scarlet anorak over a black cashmere sweater, black cords and sensible boots. As reporters had little to do with features writers and as Perry had only recently joined the paper, Elspeth barely knew him.

'Elspeth,' he said with a smile. 'You must be

cursing me for moving in on your patch. I read your pieces and they were damn good.'

'It's all right,' said Elspeth, thawing before that charming smile and noticing his eyes were green. 'Mr Johnson, can you manage a room for Mr Gaunt?'

'He's in luck. One of our guests has just checked out. If you'll just sign these forms, Mr Gaunt, I'll show you to your room.'

'I'll wait down here for you,' said Elspeth, 'and then I'll show you around.'

Elspeth began to feel quite cheerful. The idea that a murderer might be lurking about trying to kill her made her feel uneasy. Hamish Macbeth always seemed to have women around him. Let's see how he likes me being accompanied by Perry.

Perry came down. 'Right,' he said. 'Like I said, I've read all your stories as well as your features. The trouble is there doesn't seem to be anything left for me to write about. You seem to have covered it all.'

'I'll drive you down to the village and introduce you to a few people,' said Elspeth. 'Have you had much experience of journalism?'

'I got a degree in journalism from Lander University in Birmingham. They'll give you a degree in anything. Someone even got a degree in flower arrangement. Before that I got a degree in mediaeval history from Oxford. Before that I was in the army. I'm quite old to be starting out. I'm thirty-three. I haven't worked on a newspaper before.'

'So how did you land this one?' asked Elspeth, curious to know whether he would admit to his father's friendship with the editor.

'You'll hate me for this. My father is a friend of Josh Appleton.' Josh was the London editor. 'He spoke to him and next thing I knew was I had the job in Glasgow. Now you'll despise me for taking it.'

'It's really no different from what goes on in Glasgow,' said Elspeth. 'Sons of printers get jobs in reporting when they've got no aptitude whatever.'

'Well, let's see if I have any talent.'

They were just crossing the forecourt to Elspeth's car when Priscilla emerged from the gift shop. She was wearing hip-hugging jeans and high boots with a black turtleneck sweater.

'Talking about local colour,' said Perry. 'Who the hell is that?'

'That is Priscilla Halburton-Smythe, daughter of the hotel owner.'

'Is her nature as beautiful as she looks?'

Elspeth felt a pang of jealousy. Men, including Hamish, had only to look at Priscilla and they forgot that such a lowly creature as Elspeth Grant even existed.

'She's actually very kind,' said Elspeth.

'Married?'

'No.'

He adjusted the passenger seat right back in Elspeth's car to accommodate his long legs. 'I've lost interest.'

'Why?'

'If a woman looks like that and is the daughter of a hotel owner and she's not married, there's something up.'

'Are you married?'

'No. Divorced. And you?'

'Nearly once. He stood me up.'

'Useless bastard. Let's go.'

Elspeth drove straight past Priscilla, who looked as if she expected Elspeth to stop the car and introduce her.

'I'll take you down to Lochdubh,' said Elspeth, 'and we'll call at the police station first.'

'I'm dying to meet the local bobby. He's featured in quite a number of stories. I looked Lochdubh up before I left.'

Elspeth's heart really warmed to Perry when he exclaimed over the village of Lochdubh, nestled in front of the loch with the two tall mountains towering behind it. 'Why, the place is beautiful!'

Elspeth, for the first time in ages, was conscious of her appearance. She had her frizzy hair scrunched up on top of her head. She was wearing jeans that were old and baggy, and her sweater under her tweed jacket was faded black from too many washings.

'I gather they've got someone for one of the murders at least,' said Perry, 'so I'd better hurry up and write something before we're called back.'

Elspeth stopped at the police station, and they got out of the car. As they approached the kitchen door, Hamish came around from the back, an empty feed pail in his hand. He was followed by Lugs and Sonsie.

'A bobby with a pet wild cat!' marvelled Perry. 'Now, there's a bit of colour for a start.'

'No, you don't,' warned Elspeth. 'He doesn't like people knowing about that cat in case it gets taken away. Actually, it's quite tame.'

'Elspeth,' said Hamish, joining them. 'Did you see Blair or Jimmy?'

'It's all quiet. The mobile police unit wasn't on the waterfront and I suppose the press are all down at Strathbane.'

'And why aren't you there?'

'Because Daviot will make one of his pompous statements and you know what's really going on.'

'I doubt that,' said Hamish bitterly. 'Coffee?'

'Grand. This is Perry Gaunt, a feature writer. And your coffee's foul.'

'I've got round to using the percolator and I've got some decent stuff. Should be ready by now.'

Perry followed them into the kitchen. He looked around. There was a smell of peat from the stove and the aroma of fresh coffee. The round kitchen table was covered with a red-and-white gingham cloth, a present from the Italian restaurant, and gingham curtains hung at the window. Outside, the sun shone as if the Highlands had decided to give the residents a brief respite from winter.

Hamish poured mugs of coffee and then set a plate of shortbread on the table.

'I'm glad you've got company, Elspeth. I've been worried about you not being guarded.'

'Why should she be guarded?' asked Perry.

Hamish told him about the horoscopes. 'Now, there's a story!' exclaimed Perry.

'No, it's not,' snapped Elspeth. 'You should know I'm not supposed to write anything at all, other than for the *Bugle*. I can't even translate Euripides in my spare time. Hamish, surely Fergus didn't kill his wife.'

'The latest is that he sneaked out of work for two hours around the time his wife was killed and he absolutely refused to say where he was. Blair charged him with her murder, but there isn't a single bit of evidence against him. The forensic team's up at the back taking his place apart, looking for a weapon. He's got money from his wife's insurance so when they eventually allowed him a lawyer, he called in Agnes Dunne from Inverness. She'll soon have him out on bail. She's a terror. I wanted to investigate further but Blair found I had a lot of holiday time owing and he found some regulation that I had to take at least a week.

'I'm losing heart, Elspeth. I'm weary. Let me know if you get any ideas.'

'Right,' said Elspeth. 'I'll start by taking Perry here over to Braikie.'

'If you dig up anything, let me know.'

Elspeth stopped the car on the shore road outside Braikie.

'You see those houses?' she said.

'Yes, all boarded up.'

'The tide's got higher every year. At high tide, this road is flooded. You can see where it's being eaten away. A lot of the coastal villages are suffering but no one does anything. You could maybe put in a bit about that. You know the sort of thing – it's not only a murderer in their midst that the people of Sutherland dread, but another that is taking away their homes yaddity ya.'

'Got it.'

Elspeth drove on to the main street and parked. 'I'm hungry. There's a chippy. We could have fish-and-chips or haggis-and-chips or black-pudding-and-chips or . . .'

'Deep-fried Mars bars?'

'Of course. And deep-fried pizza, too.'

'You know,' said Perry, 'the average life span of a man in Glasgow is now fifty-seven, and they put it down to a diet of the stuff you've just mentioned. I want a drink. What about The Highlanders Arms over there?'

'They've got meat pies from the bakery that aren't bad.'

'We'll try that and you can tell me all about the dead postmistress.'

Perry had been damned in the Glasgow office as a 'posh git'. But Elspeth found his manner of listening intently, his light accent and his very green eyes intriguing. One read a lot about people with green eyes in books, particularly American books. Maybe green eyes weren't so unusual in the States, but it was rare to see such vivid green in Britain that was not pale or mixed with brown. Her mind turned briefly to Hamish. He blew hot and cold and any time they seemed to be getting close, he always turned away to some other woman, usually Priscilla.

'Do you really think these murders are connected?' Perry asked.

'I'm not so sure about the one at Bonar Bridge. But the others, yes. Catriona Beldame was hated, Ina probably knew something, and the silly postmistress bragged that she did.'

'Do we still write postmistress or do we have to write postperson?'

'God forbid! Mind you, there's probably some new name like post office executive manager, or something. Ellie lived above the shop. Let's go round there and see if some relative is cleaning up, someone she might have said something to.'

'You're doing Hamish Macbeth's job.'

'No, I'm doing my own. I'm a reporter, remember? You haven't eaten your pie.'

Perry looked round the dismal dirty pub. 'I'm frightened to.'

'If this frightens you, some of the places in Glasgow will scare your socks off. Come on.'

Elspeth found the street door leading to Ellie's flat standing open. They went up the stairs. The flat door was open as well. A small woman was standing in the living room putting stuff into a packing case.

'Excuse me,' said Elspeth.

The woman straightened up. She was wearing a floral pinafore over a dun-coloured sweater and dark blue polyester slacks. She was small and wiry with a pug face and grey hair.

'What do you want?'

'We're from the *Daily Bugle* . . .'

'Sod off.'

Perry moved in front of Elspeth. 'I know it must distress you to be approached by the press at such a time. But I think Miss Ellie Macpherson should be remembered not as a murder victim, but as a real, live person.' He gave his charming smile. 'More to the point, you seem to have a lot of work and we could help you.'

She looked up at him for a long moment and then to Elspeth's surprise, she smiled, exposing a set of dazzlingly white dentures. 'I could do with the help. I'm Betty Macpherson, Ellie's sister. Wouldn't think so, would you? She was aye a great beanpole o' a lass.'

'I am Perry Gaunt and this is my colleague, Elspeth Grant. Maybe we could make you a cup of tea. Then you can take a rest and tell us what to do.'

'You're right kind for an Englishman,' said Betty. 'Tea would be nice.'

'I'll get it,' said Elspeth.

When she returned from the kitchen with the tea things, Perry was on his knees, packing china ornaments. 'I don't want any of her stupid books,' said Betty. 'Witch indeed. I don't want that crystal ball, either.'

Elspeth poured tea into mugs. Then she picked up the crystal ball and gazed into it. 'Someone would pay you for this,' she said. Suddenly she was engulfed with a wave of hate, fear and anger. She dropped the ball on the carpet, where it rolled over to Perry. He looked curiously at Elspeth's white face. 'What is it?'

Elspeth shook her head as if to clear it. 'Nothing. I felt queasy. Must have been that pie.'

He picked up the ball and put it back on the table.

Elspeth wished she had brought the photographer. The crystal ball had been the murder weapon. She had her own camera in her bag, but she dreaded picking up the ball again. She wondered why forensics had released it. She thought they kept murder weapons forever.

'I'm surprised they gave that thing back to you,' she said, pointing to the ball.

'Oh, that's not the murder weapon,' said Betty. 'I wouldn't have such a thing around. She must have had the two. If you think I could get any money for it, pack it up.'

'I hope this is not too painful for you,' said Elspeth, 'but did your sister tell you anything that might lead you to suspect she knew the murderer?'

'We didnae talk much. We were aye like chalk and cheese. I think Ellie should have gone on the stage and got it out of her system. She would tell any lie to get attention. I mind when she was just a wee lass, her opening the fridge door and standing there in the light from the fridge, graciously inclining her head as if accepting an award.

'This is what comes of her lies.' A tear rolled down Betty's cheek.

'Drink your tea,' said Perry, 'and I'll get on with packing things up.'

Now that there seemed nothing further to find out, Elspeth could only marvel at Perry's patience as he deftly wrapped kitchen stuff and other odds and ends and put them into packing cases.

When they eventually left, Perry said, 'Now I really am starving.'

'Let's go back to the hotel,' said Elspeth. 'Clarry, the chef, will rustle something up for you.'

Hamish was sitting in the lounge with Priscilla when Elspeth and Perry entered. Elspeth's face was flushed and her eyes were shining. Her face fell when she saw Priscilla. She waited for the inevitable. Perry would forget all about her and be fascinated by Priscilla.

She introduced Perry to Priscilla and said, 'Perry's desperate for something to eat.'

Priscilla rose to her feet. 'What about soup and a plate of sandwiches?'

'That would be great.'

'I'll tell Clarry.'

When Priscilla had left, Elspeth said, 'I thought you'd be out trying to find out where Fergus really was.'

'We were just going over my notes,' said Hamish defensively. Perry and Elspeth sat down.

'Could he have been with a woman?' asked Elspeth. 'He wouldn't want to say so, would he? I mean with his wife just dead.'

Hamish stared at her for a long moment. 'The brothel,' he said. 'What if Fergus was one of Fiona McNulty's clients? He wouldn't have the time to go all the way over to Bonar Bridge. And she was still in Cnothan when Ina was murdered. Maybe he went to Cnothan where she used to be. I'll get down to the newspaper and get a photograph of him from Matthew and see if anyone over there saw him.'

He almost expected Elspeth to volunteer to go with him, but she said 'Good idea' and settled back in her chair.

Having secured a photograph, Hamish was driving towards Cnothan when his mobile phone rang. He stopped at the side of the road and answered it. It was Lesley. 'This is short notice, Hamish,' she said. 'I wonder whether you would like to come over to my place tonight for dinner?'

Hamish thought rapidly. Priscilla was as

cool as ever, and Elspeth seemed enamoured of the feature writer. 'What time?' he asked.

'Eight o'clock. Here's the address.'

Hamish wrote it down. 'See you then,' he said, and rang off.

He drove up to where the mobile home used to be and once more called at the croft where the gnome-like man lived. He showed him Fergus's photograph but the man shook his head.

Hamish tried several of the other outlying crofts but without success. The trouble was, he thought, that to get to the mobile home, Fergus would not have needed to go through the town.

Then he had an idea. If Fergus had been in the habit of visiting Fiona, would he have known that she would have a supply of condoms, or, on his first visit, would he call in at the chemist in Cnothan to get a packet?

He drove into town and went to the chemist. The pharmacist, Mr Hepworth, was standing behind the counter with a young female assistant. Hamish showed them the photograph of Fergus and asked if they could remember him ever buying condoms.

Mr Hepworth shook his head but the girl giggled and said, 'Oh, I mind him.'

'Tell me about it,' urged Hamish.

'He looked around for a long time. Then he bought toothpaste. Then he wandered around again. The condoms are right here on the counter. He kept staring at them as he was paying for the toothpaste and his face was bright red and he was sweating although it was a cold day. I took pity on him so I picked up a packet and said, "Can I wrap this for you as well?" He said, "Aye," paid for them, and fairly fled out of the shop. I mind it well 'cos I had a good laugh about it with my friends that evening.'

'When was this?' asked Hamish.

'Last September. I can't remember the exact day.'

Hamish took a note of her name and address and then left, deep in thought.

Fergus had been in the habit of visiting Fiona. That was where he might have been on the afternoon his wife was being murdered.

He went back to the police station, collected Sonsie and Lugs, and drove to Strathbane.

He stopped in the car park and phoned Jimmy. 'What is it?' asked Jimmy. 'I've finished for the day and I want to get to the pub.'

'I'll meet you there.'

In the pub, Jimmy listened carefully and then said bitterly, 'Trust you to throw a spanner in the works. If you want to make my life even more miserable, talk to her.'

He pointed to a woman at a corner table who was working on a laptop. 'That's Fergus's lawyer, Agnes Dunne. She's all set to get him out on bail. I'll just stay here and get drunk.'

Hamish approached Agnes Dunne. She was a hatchet-faced woman in her forties wearing a power suit.

'Yes?' she demanded.

Hamish sat down opposite her and told her about Fergus's visits to Fiona. 'Get him to say that's where he was and if he told anyone at work where he was going and if he maybe went into the town afterwards and might have been seen in one of the shops.'

She switched off her laptop and closed it down. 'Come with me,' she said, 'although I hope they don't try to pin the murder at Bonar Bridge on him now.'

Jimmy swallowed his drink and went with them. To Hamish's relief, Blair was nowhere in sight. The duty officer led the way down to the cells in the basement.

Fergus was sitting with his head in his hands. He looked up when they entered.

Hamish sat down on the bed and faced him.

'You're a right fool, Fergus. Why didn't you just tell the truth? I now know you were visiting Fiona McNulty.'

'You cannae tell anyone, Hamish,' exclaimed Fergus. 'Oh, man, the shame o' it. They'll never let me inside the kirk again.'

'Listen to me, Fergus. You have been charged with the murder of your wife. I am sure they are trying to pin the other murders on you as well. You'll spend the rest of your life in prison if you don't speak up now. Now, on the day of Ina's murder, did you go to Fiona?'

'Aye,' he mumbled.

'Now, think very carefully. Did you go into the village?'

'Aye, I did that. I'll never forget it. I thocht she might say something.'

'Who? Where?'

'It was after . . . you know . . . I went into that café on the main street and I ordered a mutton pie and peas and some tea.' He looked at Hamish with a sort of bewildered innocence. 'It makes ye hungry.'

'Sex?'

'Aye. That lassie, Sky – stupit name – herself was serving. She says, "My dad says you're getting to be a regular around these parts." I was that feart, I leapt to my feet and knocked the teapot on to the floor. I threw some money on the table and ran for it.'

'You see how simple it is?' said Hamish. 'I'll get over there right now and check it out.'

* * *

Lesley looked with pride at her dinner table. It was set with her finest china and a bottle of good claret nestled in its basket, ready to pour. She had brushed her red-gold hair until it shone. She was wearing a white silk blouse with a low neckline and her late mother's pearls. Pearl drops hung from her small ears. A black velvet skirt went to ankle length, just showing a pair of high-heeled black patent shoes with thin straps. She was wearing a scarlet thong and wriggled a little with the discomfort of it.

Lesley went into the bathroom and sprayed herself with Givenchy's Hot. Eight o'clock came and went. She began to pace up and down. She was just about to phone Hamish when the doorbell rang.

She opened the door and stared at Hamish. He was wearing his uniform, and his dog and cat were at his feet.

'What are they doing here?' she demanded, pointing at the animals.

'I'm right sorry, Lesley. I didn't have time to take them home. They're right hungry and they need some water. If you wouldnae mind . . .'

She slammed the door in his face, rushed into the bathroom, and glared in fury at her reflection in the mirror.

'The man's a hick!' she screamed. Now she felt she knew why this man had avoided promotion. He was nothing more than a highland peasant. She had gone to all this trouble. Not only had he turned up in his shabby uniform but he'd had the cheek to bring along his weird pets and expect her to feed them!

Hamish stood outside the door. He wondered whether to knock again and ask her what on earth was up with her. Then he shrugged. He was tired and hungry. He helped Sonsie and Lugs into the Land Rover. 'Don't you worry,' he said. 'We'll find a chippy.'

He was pleased with the day's work. Sky had remembered the incident and had also remembered the day because that had been the day of her birthday. Fergus was a lucky man. Strathbane might consider themselves back to square one but Hamish had the advantage of never having believed Fergus guilty in the first place.

He bought Sonsie a fish supper at the chip shop, and as a treat he bought Lugs a black pudding supper. Lugs was partial to black pudding. He also bought two bottles of mineral water. He settled for a haggis supper for himself.

He drove up out of Strathbane and stopped on the moors. He poured the mineral water into bowls for his pets before eating his deep-fried slice of haggis and his chips.

He was too tired to really worry about what was up with Lesley. As he drove off again, he saw flakes of snow beginning to dance in front of the windscreen. At first they swirled down hypnotically, but as he gained the bridge into Lochdubh, the snow was blowing horizontally on a screaming gale.

He was glad to be home. He lit the stove and settled down at the kitchen table with a glass of whisky. He decided that in the morning, he would go over all the reports and see if there was anything he had missed.

Elspeth twisted and turned that night, unable to get to sleep. She felt she was falling in love with Perry. She knew in her Gypsy soul that one can always pull back before it is too late and yet her very interest in Perry had freed her from any thoughts about Hamish Macbeth – and it was great to be free of that. Let the poor idiot remain enraptured by Priscilla until the end of his days. She just didn't care any more.

The gale screamed around the hotel. She was in one of the turret rooms, and it appeared to be getting the main force of the wind.

Elspeth decided to try to read herself to sleep. She switched on the bedside light. It was covered by a dainty rose-coloured fringed shade and did not give much illumination. She thought it would be a good idea to get out of bed and switch on the overhead light.

Then she stared at the door. Her heart started to beat fast. She could swear someone was slowly turning the handle.

She picked up the phone. The line was dead. She knew she had locked the door, but what if someone was prepared to break it open or had found a pass key?

Elspeth scrambled out of bed and searched in her handbag for her mobile. She switched it on. The little screen said no signal. The storm must have damaged reception from the local mobile phone tower.

There was only one thing for it. Elspeth screamed and screamed, hoping her screams might be heard above the roar of the storm.

A sound of running feet. A banging at the door. Perry's blessed voice shouting, 'Are you all right?'

Elspeth hurtled to the door and opened it. 'Thank God!' she cried and threw herself into Perry's arms.

'What the matter?' he asked.

'I saw the door handle turn and thought the murderer had come for me!'

'Let's phone the police.'

'The phones are down and Hamish would never get up here in this blizzard.'

'If it was someone, and if Hamish can't get

up here, then whoever it was can't get away. Come on. Let's get downstairs.'

Elspeth put on a dressing gown and slippers. She thought illogically, Why am I wearing a pair of striped pyjamas and this ratty old dressing gown? I ought to be wearing something from Victoria's Secret.

Perry took her hand in a warm clasp and they hurried down the stairs. The night porter was asleep at the desk.

'Wake up!' said Perry, shaking him. 'Someone's tried to attack Miss Grant and that person might still be in the hotel. Hit the fire alarm. Get everyone down here.'

Mr Johnson and Priscilla were the first to arrive. Priscilla was wearing a long pale green silk dressing gown that seemed to have been moulded to her figure. She did not have a hair out of place. Perry quickly explained what was wrong.

Other guests gathered in the hall and then some hungover reporters and photographers and the few members of the staff who lived in.

'Someone tried to get into Miss Grant's room,' said Mr Johnson. 'I want you all to search the hotel to see if you can find a stranger. Also keep looking out of the upper windows in case someone is trying to escape through the snow.'

The hotel was searched from top to bottom. It took a long time because the old building was full of unexpected nooks and cupboards and storerooms.

Everyone ended up in the hall again, weary and cross, some reporters saying loudly that it was probably Perry trying to get into Elspeth's knickers.

'You better share my room for the rest of the night,' said Perry. 'It's got twin beds.'

'It's all right,' said Priscilla. 'There's a free room next to mine.'

I really am beginning to hate you, thought Elspeth, but she smiled and said, 'Perry and I have stories to discuss. I'll share his room.'

When Elspeth settled into the twin bed in Perry's room, she said in a small voice, 'Do you think I was imagining things?'

'I heard one of the maids say you were psychic. Did you sense anything?'

'No. I get strange feelings from time to time but I can't seem to conjure them up when I need them.'

'It'll be all right. We'll try to get to the police station in the morning. Go to sleep.'

If this were a romance, thought Elspeth, he would take me in his arms and say he would protect me for the rest of his life. A few minutes later, Perry let out a gentle snore. So much for romance! Elspeth turned on her side and drifted down into a dream where a dark figure was chasing her along endless corridors.

Priscilla was thinking of Perry. He was so attractive and so suitable. He was everything Hamish Macbeth was not. She wondered if there was anything going on with Elspeth. Elspeth often looked as if she bought her clothes exclusively in the cheapest type of charity shop, but there was no denying that men did seem to be attracted to her.

I'll need to think up some way to have him to myself, thought Priscilla. Elspeth's bound to go off on her own sometime or other.

Lesley sighed with relief when she reached the forensic lab the following morning. She'd had to walk to work because the streets of Strathbane had not yet been cleared. Bruce, the head of the lab, was the only other person there.

'The lazy sods are using the snow as an excuse not to come to work,' he complained as Lesley pulled off her boots and put on a pair of dry flat shoes. 'Well, that's Fergus Braid off the hook.'

'What?'

'I was in the pub last night. Blair was furious, trying to say Macbeth made it up.'

'What are you talking about?'

'Last evening Macbeth found a witness over in Cnothan who had seen Fergus at the time of his wife's murder.'

'Did you say yesterday evening?'

'Yes. Why?'

'Just wondered.' Lesley bit her lip in vexation. So that was why he had still been in uniform and had brought those wretched animals with him. He must be furious with her. She decided to phone him.

'The phones aren't working and in case you haven't noticed, we haven't any electricity, either,' said Bruce. 'There's nothing we can do until the power comes on.'

'Haven't we got a generator?'

'No,' lied Bruce, who had in fact borrowed it for his home during an earlier power cut and forgotten to bring it back.

On the same clear and very cold morning, Elspeth and Perry borrowed skis and managed to make their way to the police station.

Hamish listened intently. He knew Elspeth well enough not to accuse her of imagining things. When Elspeth and Perry had finished talking, he said, 'I can't understand how someone would get up to the hotel in a raging blizzard unless it was one of the guests. Which guests who were here at the murder of Catriona are still at the hotel?'

'I don't know,' said Elspeth.

'But I do,' said Priscilla from the doorway. Elspeth scowled. She saw the way Priscilla looked at Perry. Couldn't that damn female leave her just one man?

'Who are they?' asked Hamish.

'Just the one. A Mr Garry.'

'We checked on him.' Hamish had piles of papers spread out in front of him on the table. 'Ah, here we are! Mr Dominic Garry. Stockbroker. Likes hill walking. Fifty-five years old. He's pretty fit?'

'Yes. He's tall and thin. Does a lot of walking. He borrowed the last of the skis so I don't suppose he'll be going anywhere today.'

'I'll get up to the hotel and have a word with him.'

'We'd better get started on your colour piece, Perry,' said Elspeth. 'We'll go along to the *Highland Times* and use a desk there.'

'I heard the snow plough going past,' said Priscilla. 'You might be able to get up there in the Land Rover, Hamish. I'll come with you.'

As they arrived at the hotel forecourt, Priscilla said, 'That's Mr Garry. Just leaving.'

Hamish jumped down from the Land Rover and called out, 'Mr Garry! A word with you!'

Garry was wearing an expensive anorak over thick knee breeches and sturdy boots.

'I was just going out for a walk,' he said. 'Isn't it beautiful in the snow?'

'If you wouldn't mind coming back into the hotel. It won't take long,' said Hamish.

When they were seated in a corner of the lounge, Hamish waited until Garry had shrugged off his anorak and said, 'As you will have heard, Mr Garry, there have been murders committed.'

'And what's that got to do with me?'

'I am just asking everyone around if they might have seen anything,' said Hamish soothingly. 'Now, I see from my notes that you are a stockbroker from London. I am curious as to why you are up here on such a long holiday. This hotel is expensive.'

'Do I have to tell you?'

Hamish's eyes sharpened. 'Of course.'

'I had a nervous breakdown. You can check with my psychiatrist. I'll give you his number. He suggested I take a long break as far away from London as possible. I have plenty of money, and this has been a very healing experience.'

'What caused the breakdown?'

'I was wrongly accused of insider trading. By the time my name was cleared and I was settling down, my wife asked for a divorce. Come up to my room. I am going to give you phone numbers to check my story and then will you please leave me alone? I will also telephone my psychiatrist and give him permission to speak to you. I gather the phones are working again.'

Hamish, when he got back to the police station, telephoned the psychiatrist. As he listened, his heart sank. He had been hoping that it would turn out some crazed outsider had been responsible. But the psychiatrist confirmed that Garry had indeed had a nervous breakdown. He said that in his opinion, Garry was a gentle man, not suited for the cut-throat life of the City. The divorce had been the final straw. He had private means. He warned Hamish not to upset him.

Hamish gloomily went back to studying his notes. Surely somewhere in the middle of all this information was something he had missed.

His eyes fell on the statement he had taken from Timmy Teviot. The man hadn't been lying about the poachers, but there had been something else he hadn't been saying. There had been something at the back of his eyes, and Hamish was suddenly sure he knew about the brothel.

Timmy wouldn't be working today. The road right round the loch wouldn't be cleared yet, but he decided to put his skis on and call on Timmy.

The phone rang. It was Lesley. 'Hamish, I am very sorry . . . ,' she was beginning.

'Talk to you later,' said Hamish. 'Got to rush,' and put the phone down.

The phone immediately rang again.

'I told you . . .,' Hamish was beginning when Elspeth's voice came down the line.

'It's me, Elspeth. Hamish, while Perry was writing his piece, I've been thinking and thinking about the murders. The one thing that seems to tie them all together is sex.'

'Sex!'

'Think about it.'

Chapter Ten

The beaten men come into their own.
– John Masefield

After a long and weary trudge round the loch, Hamish was irritated to be told that Timmy had gone to the pub in Lochdubh.

The ground round the loch was flat, so there were no slopes to ski down. He wished he had worn his snowshoes instead. The sun was glittering blindingly on the snow. Lochdubh looked like a Christmas card, but, that morning, he was in no mood to admire it. When he reached the cleared waterfront, he took off his skis, carried them to the police station and propped them against the wall. Then he made his way to the pub.

He went straight up to Timmy, who was propping up the bar. 'You,' said Hamish curtly. 'Follow me to the station.'

To Timmy's nervous demands of 'What's

up? What have I done?' Hamish only replied, 'In the station.'

When they were settled in the office, Hamish began. 'You've been holding out on me, Timmy.'

'Me? Man, I tellt ye about them poachers.'

'So you did. But you didn't tell me you knew about Fiona McNulty.'

There was something like relief at the back of Timmy eyes. 'Oh, well, I didn't want to go getting any of the men in the village into trouble.'

'Like Fergus?'

'Aye, he was the only one I knew about.'

'And how did you know about him?'

'We got drinking one night and he tellt me.'

Hamish's eyes sharpened. 'There's something else he told you that you aren't letting on. Out with it, Timmy, or I'll take you down to Strathbane and let Blair deal with you.'

'I cannae go betraying the man's confidence.'

'Then we're off to see Blair.'

'Och, anything but that. But you didnae hear it from me!'

'Out with it.'

'I cannae think it's got anything to do wi' the murder o' his poor wife.'

'Spit it out.'

'It sounds right daft now. But she used to beat him.'

'Ina? That wee woman?'

'Fact. He had a sore dunt tae the head and he was saying it happened at work, but when he'd had a few jars, he says tae me that Ina hit him wi' the frying pan.'

'Why did she do that?' asked Hamish.

'She'd learned from one o' the women that he'd been seen one night up at the witch's place.'

'You should ha' told me this before. Off with you, Timmy. I may be talking to you later.'

Hamish phoned Jimmy. 'I thought you were supposed to be on holiday,' said Jimmy.

'I am. Is Fergus out?'

'Yes, he's at home.'

'Thanks.'

'Hamish, if you know anything . . .'

'I'll let you know. Talk to you later.'

Hamish walked up to Fergus's home and knocked at the door. Fergus answered. 'Not again,' he said. 'I'm no' going back tae Strathbane.'

'Just a wee chat,' said Hamish.

'Come ben.'

Hamish edged his way around bulging rubbish sacks on the front step. 'Been cleaning?' he asked.

'Aye. When I came back and saw the mess I'd been living in, I couldnae bear the sight of it. Poor Ina would ha' gone mad.'

Hamish took off his cap and sat down. 'Fergus, did Ina beat you?'

'What a thing to say and her not cold in her grave!'

'Fergus. You've got into trouble by not telling the truth. Out with it.'

'Well, maybe,' Fergus mumbled.

'You were seen going to Catriona Beldame's.'

'Och, that was silly. She gave me this stuff and all it did was make my balls itch.'

'And Ina found out you'd been there?'

'Yes, someone told her.'

'And what did she do?'

'She hit me with the frying pan.'

'And was she in the habit of hitting you?'

Fergus hung his head. Then he burst out with: 'What could I do, Hamish? I couldnae hit a woman. I couldnae talk about it. Me, a big man being hit by a wee woman? The shame o' it.'

'What about Fiona McNulty. Did Ina know about her?'

'Maybe.'

'What maybe?'

'The day she was murdered, she left a note for me.'

'Fergus. For God's sake, man. The things you've been keeping from me. Have you got the note?'

'No, I burnt it.'

'What did it say?'

'It said something like, "I know what you've been up to and you're for it."'

'I got the idea you were relieved when she was killed.'

'I was that. I'm free at last. That's what I thought. But you know what it's like. You read about old lags who feel so strange and lost when they're let out of prison after a long sentence that they can't wait to get in again. I don't seem to have thought for myself or acted for myself for a long time.'

'But you went to Fiona.'

Fergus looked at Hamish with pleading eyes. 'Fiona wasnae really a hoor. She just did a bit on the side for some fellows. She was warm and nice. Hamish, you may as well have the lot. I hadn't had any sex since my honeymoon. When we got back, herself says, "I'm not having any more of that nastiness."'

'You had grounds for a divorce.'

'This is Lochdubh, Hamish. I'm not the only one.'

'Who else visited Fiona?'

'I don't know and that's the truth. I never asked her. I wanted to keep up the lie that she was mine only.'

Fergus began to cry, great gulping sobs. Hamish handed him a handkerchief and waited in sympathetic silence until Fergus had cried himself out. 'Just look at me,' said

Fergus. 'Crying over a hoor when I cannae even shed a tear for my ain wife.'

'Here's what I want you to do,' said Hamish. 'I want you to go to Dr Brodie and get him to recommend a good psychiatrist. You need to talk all this out.'

'I'm not mad!'

'No, but you'll drive yourself mad wi' the load o' guilt you're carrying. Now, do you have any idea who's been committing these murders?'

'Hamish, I swear to God I haven't a clue.'

Elspeth was wondering what to do about Perry. They both had been summoned back to the office. Elspeth had pointed out that the roads south were still impassable in a lot of places. The news editor told her to get back as soon as she could and to bring Perry with her.

She was anxious to remove Perry from Priscilla's orbit. Perry was easy and charming to both of them. Elspeth was only comforted by the fact that she had overheard Priscilla inviting Perry for dinner and Perry had refused, saying he still had work to do.

In order to get Perry out of the hotel, she suggested they go down to the police station. 'It would be a shame,' said Elspeth, 'to get on the road and then find out Hamish had solved the murders. Then we've got Catriona's funeral later on.'

'Do you think he will solve the murders?' asked Perry.

'He always has in the past. Mind you, there's a first time for everything.'

Hamish was in his office. He had pinned a large sheet of paper up on the wall with the names of the four murdered women with arrows pointing to each name from a centre circle in which he had written the one word in heavy black ink – SEX.

'Come in,' he said. 'I'm just trying to work something out. Now, Archie Maclean said to me, "We don't do sex in Lochdubh." I thought that was funny at the time. But think of it. If that's the case, there must be a good few sexually repressed men around.'

'Including you,' said Elspeth.

'Don't be cheeky. Let me think. Wait a bit. What if I've been looking at this the wrong way round?'

'The funeral's today,' interrupted Elspeth.

'Whose funeral?'

'Catriona. She's still legally married to Rory so he's agreed to stump up. Don't suppose any of the village will be going, but Perry and I may as well do a piece. Mrs Wellington will be there, of course.'

'That's it!' exclaimed Hamish. 'Mrs Wellington. The village women were complaining to her about Catriona. What if I should be looking for a woman instead of a man? Take Catriona's murder. Lesley said that provided the weapon was sharp enough, then a woman could have done it. All the murders seem to have been done in a frenzy of hate. Now, if Ina wasn't one of the murderees, I might have thought it was her.'

'Why Ina?'

'Never you mind. When's the funeral?'

'Three o'clock.'

'Maybe see you there. I've got to dash.'

As Hamish walked up to the manse, he marvelled at how little he actually knew of what went on behind the lace curtains of the cottages in Lochdubh.

Whoever would have thought that Fergus was a battered husband?

Mrs Wellington greeted him with a curt, 'I'm busy.'

'It iss verra important,' said Hamish. Mrs Wellington always made him feel nervous. She invited him into the manse's vast and old-fashioned kitchen.

'Don't sit down,' she barked as Hamish removed his hat.

He turned and faced her. 'Before Catriona

was murdered, a lot of the women came to you about their husbands visiting her. Was there any particular one that was more upset than the others?'

'If, as I think you are, you are trying to pin any of these murders on the respectable ladies of Lochdubh, then I have nothing to say to you.'

'There have been four murders and maybe they'll be another one if you don't help.'

'Then look for a man! Women are the gentler sex, or have you forgotten?'

'Did you know that Ina Braid beat her husband?'

Mrs Wellington had been rolling pastry. She glared at him and brandished the rolling pin. Hamish took a quick step back.

'Either Fergus is really guilty or all this has turned his brain. I knew Ina Braid, and she was a gentle soul.'

Hamish returned to the station. The wind was rising and blowing powdery snow from the tops of drifts. The sky above was getting darker. Villagers were queuing at Patel's, frightened that more snow would mean that deliveries of goods wouldn't get through.

In the police station, he sought out two camper's gas lamps and placed them in readiness on the kitchen table. More snow would probably mean a power cut. Sonsie and Lugs crashed through the flap on the door. Hamish could see that their coats were embedded with hard little snowballs. He filled a basin with warm water and patiently began to remove the snow from them.

Then he put more peat in the stove before pouring himself a cup of coffee, going into the office, getting his notes, and once more spreading them out on the kitchen table.

The snow meant that he would have at least the whole of what was left of the day free from interruptions. Then he remembered Catriona's funeral. Surely it wouldn't take place on such a day.

He phoned Mrs Wellington. 'No, of course not,' she said in answer to his query. 'Mr McBride is unable to get further north because of the snow and we are going to wait until he arrives.'

'What . . .?' began Hamish when the phone went dead.

He went back to the kitchen and tried the lights. No success. The snow piling up against the kitchen window was cutting out any light.

He lit the lamps and hoped that his sheep were safely in the shelter he had built for them. He suddenly cursed, remembering he hadn't given them their winter feed.

Hamish strapped on his snowshoes and collected two buckets of feed he had ready by the door. He put on a coat and woollen hat, opened the door and plunged into the roaring white storm outside. He felt a superstitious shudder as he made his way up the hill at the back.

The wind was screaming and howling. It was as if the old gods had decided to take back Sutherland, take it away from the petty grip of man and restore it to a wilderness.

He was pleased that the low wooden shelter he had built for the sheep was holding up. He poured their feed into a trough, stood for a moment watching them, and then headed back to the station.

Elspeth and Perry struggled back to the hotel. 'We'll never get out of here,' said Perry. 'Not that I care much.' But that charming smile of his was not only for Elspeth but also for Priscilla, who had come to meet them.

'Clarry's made some mulled wine,' said Priscilla. 'Like some?'

'Lovely,' said Perry. 'Wait till we get out of these wet clothes. My feet feel like two blocks of ice and we're dripping melted snow all over the place. Come on, Elspeth.'

Priscilla watched them go. Was there anything going on between them? Her father had got on the phone to friends in the south and had found out all about Perry's impeccable background and had started nagging his daughter to 'do something'.

Usually that would have been enough to put Priscilla off, but she was becoming more and more fascinated by Perry.

The hotel generator could be heard faintly through the noise of the storm outside. She paced up and down the hall. What was taking them so long? Had they gone to bed together? Perish the thought!

Priscilla decided that she had better retreat to the lounge and look as if she were reading a magazine.

It was a full half-hour before they both appeared.

'I'll get the wine,' said Priscilla.

'Don't you just ring the bell?' asked Perry.

'Only a few of the staff live in, and they are cleaning the rooms.'

'She moves like a dancer,' said Perry appreciatively. 'Very graceful girl.'

'I brought down my laptop,' said Elspeth in a dull little voice. 'I thought that after we have had our mulled wine, we could go though everything. There might be a clue somewhere.'

'All right. At least if someone wants to kill you, they won't get anywhere near the hotel in this weather.'

'Something's up!' Elspeth cocked her head to one side like a bird. Then she ran out of the lounge, through the hall and out the open door. Very faintly, muffled by the roar of the storm, she heard the church bell. But it couldn't be ringing for Catriona. She had already checked that the funeral was off. The bell, apart from Sundays, was only rung for an emergency.

This she told to Perry who had appeared beside her. 'I'd better get back down there,' she said. 'There might be a story. I'll get the photographer.'

'Elspeth, I am not going out into that screaming wilderness again.'

'Suit yourself.'

The emergency was that Mr Patel's small son, Bertie, had gone missing. In answer to his frantic cries for help, Hamish had rushed to the church and rung the bell, telling the village men who had struggled to answer its summons to start searching. He then did a quick check of the bedroom that Bertie shared with his brothers. On Bertie's pillow was an open book, the story of the Ice Queen.

Bertie was only six years old and a dreamy boy. Had he gone out to look for the mythical queen?

Priscilla came back with a tray of mulled wine. 'Where's Elspeth?'

'Our intrepid reporter thought she heard the church bell ringing. Her photographer is refusing to move.'

Priscilla put down the tray. 'I'll go after her. She shouldn't be on her own. And something serious must have happened.'

'Now I feel like a heel,' said Perry. 'I'll come with you.'

Elspeth skied towards the village. She was halfway there when she realized the wind was slacking. She dug her poles in and came to an abrupt stop. Something was lying on the road.

She went forward. It was a child. A faint whimper escaped it.

Elspeth dragged the child to its feet. A tear-stained brown face looked up at her.

'You're Patel's boy,' said Elspeth. 'What are . . .? Never mind. I'm going to stoop down and I want you to get on my back. Right. Now hang on very tightly and I'll get you home.'

She dug in her poles and sped down the road, nearly taking off at the humpbacked bridge.

Elspeth went straight to Patel's. Mrs Patel burst into tears as her boy slid down off Elspeth's back.

'Get blankets,' said Elspeth. 'I'll go and get Dr Brodie.'

Word spread rapidly that the boy had been found. Matthew Campbell had taken a photograph of Elspeth as she sped into the village with the boy on her back. He would add it to his stories about the blizzard and send a copy out to the nationals.

By the time Elspeth returned with Dr Brodie, the shop was full of people, including Perry and Priscilla. A grateful Mr Patel hugged Elspeth, tears of gratitude running down his cheeks. 'Bertie had been reading a story about the Ice Queen. He asked me where she lived. He said he had seen her in the shop. He meant you, Miss Halburton-Smythe, because you look like the pictures in his book. So I said that she lived in that big castle up on the hill.'

'Take me upstairs to the boy,' said Dr Brodie.

Hamish had been standing listening. He suddenly laughed. 'The Ice Queen! That is a verra good description.'

'Shut up!' said Priscilla and walked out of the shop.

The following morning Hamish went back to studying his notes and reports until his head ached. If the murderer was a woman, then he was looking at someone in the village. He went back to the old guest list for the hotel. No hope there.

Then he went into the office and looked at the chart on the wall. Four murders all leading down to the sign that read SEX.

Wait a minute, he thought. Have I been missing the obvious? The one person with a clear motive is Fergus. What if Sky in the café had been lying? Or what if she wanted a bit of the limelight? That was the trouble with so many reality programmes on television – everyone wanted fame these days without necessarily working at anything to achieve it. Maybe she had seen herself called as a witness at a murder trial and being photographed afterwards.

Hamish wondered if the roads had been ploughed all the way over to Cnothan.

He dressed warmly, got into the Land Rover, and drove off. He was in luck. The roads had been ploughed. The sun was low in the sky. It never rose very high in the winter. He parked in the main street and entered the café. The owner said it was Sky's day off, but that she lived in the last house at the top of the main street.

Hamish went there and rang the bell. A thin, faded blonde woman wearing too much make-up answered the door. 'I am Police Constable Macbeth from Lochdubh,' said Hamish. 'Might I be having a wee word with Sky?'

'What's she done?'

'Nothing as far as I know,' said Hamish mildly. 'Am I talking to Sky's mother?'

'Yes.'

'When's her birthday?'

'Tenth o' June. Why are you asking?'

Hamish's heart felt suddenly heavy. 'Never mind. Just call her.'

'Go in and have a seat. I'll get her.'

After a few moments, Sky slouched in. She was a sulky-looking girl, chewing a great wad of gum. Her hair was dyed an improbable red and she was thin to the point of anorexia.

'You lied to me,' said Hamish severely.

'I did not. I 'member that fellow fine.'

'It was not your birthday for a start. Your birthday was in June.'

'I just said that to make you believe me. But he was in that day, honest.'

'So what makes you sure it was that day?'

'I was going to go clubbing in Strathbane that evening but the mist got so bad, me and my friends didn't go.'

'There have been other foggy days,' said Hamish severely. 'You shouldnae ever lie to the police. If I find out Fergus wasnae in your café, I'll be back to arrest you for wasting police time.'

Hamish drove back to Lochdubh. He parked on the waterfront and walked up to Fergus's cottage.

Fergus ushered him in. 'A dram, Hamish?'

'No. This is serious. That girl at the café, she lied about the day she saw you being her birthday. Did you get to her in any way? Pay her?'

'Hamish, what are you talking about? I was there!'

'I'm right worried, Fergus. The one thing that connects the four women in a way is you. You stood to gain money if your husband-beating wife died. You visited Catriona and Fiona.'

'Och, Hamish. Will this never end?'

'I'll need to go over all your alibis again. I'll go to that paper mill tomorrow and warn that foreman if he's been lying for you, I'll have him arrested.'

Fergus looked weary. 'Do what you must. I've had enough. I've protested ma innocence over and over again. I'm going to phone the lawyer. I need protection.'

'I think you do.' Hamish turned in the doorway. A sudden thought struck him. Looking back at Fergus, he couldn't believe the man guilty of anything.

'Fergus, do you know of any other man in Lochdubh who's being beaten by his wife?'

Fergus gave a harsh laugh. 'Try next door.'

'What, the Framonts? Why didn't you tell me this?'

'It's husband beating. It's no' murder.'

* * *

Hamish stood outside Fergus's house. Could it be? Could it possibly be?

He went to the Framonts' and rang the bell. Colin answered the door. He had a burn mark on the side of his face.

'How did you get that burn?' asked Hamish.

'Got it at work,' said Colin.

'Can I come in? I'd like a word with you and the wife?'

'Tilly's not here.'

'Where is she?'

'She's gone up to the hotel.'

'Why?'

'Women's stuff. She wants Elspeth Grant to read her horoscope.'

Hamish stared at him and then wheeled about and began to run down to his Land Rover as fast as he could.

He drew out his mobile phone as soon as he got into the vehicle. No signal. He put on the siren and raced off out of the village.

Mr Johnson phoned Elspeth, who was working in her room. 'Mrs Framont is at the reception. She wants to come up and see you.'

'Why?'

'She wants her horoscope read.'

Elspeth felt gooseflesh rising on her arms. 'Tell her to wait in the lounge. I'll be down soon. First, has the colonel got an old flak jacket anywhere?'

'He's away but I'll ask Priscilla.'

'Tell her to phone me if she's got one.'

'What . . .?'

'Please just do it.'

Elspeth waited nervously. She tried the phone. Still dead.

Then there was a knock at the door. 'Who is it?' she called.

'It's me, Priscilla.'

Elspeth opened the door. 'What do you want with this?' asked Priscilla, holding out an old flak jacket.

'Help me on with it and I'll tell you.'

Elspeth entered the lounge. She was wearing the flak jacket under an old sweater. Fortunately the colonel had last worn his flak jacket years ago when he was a slim young officer.

'Miss Grant,' said Tilly. 'I'm right sorry to bother you but I mind you from the days when you did the horoscopes for the *Highland Times* and I wonder if I could have a reading.'

'Please sit down. No, sit opposite me. I don't do readings.' Elspeth had a sudden inspiration. 'But I read palms. Hold out your hands.'

All the while Elspeth was thinking, She can't be a murderer. She looks so small and inoffensive. But Tilly's eyes were glittering with an odd light. She held out her hands.

Hamish had nearly reached the hotel when he saw the lights of a car racing towards him. He slowed down and saw that Priscilla was the driver. He stopped. She climbed out of her car, shouting, 'Tilly Framont's at the hotel getting Elspeth to tell her horoscope.'

'I know,' Hamish shouted back. 'Let me past.'

Priscilla swung her car to the side of the one-track road and Hamish roared off past her.

Elspeth stared down at the pair of housework-reddened hands and said, 'I see violence and murder in your hands, Mrs Framont.'

Three guests came into the lounge. Tilly snatched her hands away. 'You're nothing but a fraud,' she said. She got up and began to march away. Elspeth followed her. She desperately wanted Tilly to do or say something to betray herself. Tilly went out of the hotel and walked towards her car.

'Well, goodnight,' said Elspeth, and she turned to walk back into the hotel.

A police siren sounded. Driving into the hotel, Hamish Macbeth thought he would never forget the sight that met his eyes.

As Elspeth turned away, Tilly took a pair of scissors out of her pocket, ran forward, and stabbed Elspeth viciously in the back.

Elspeth fell face forward in the snow.

Hamish jumped down from the Land Rover and grabbed Tilly and threw her to the ground. She screamed and clawed at him. He finally got handcuffs on her. Mr Johnson came running out. Priscilla drove up and got out of her car. She and Hamish ran to Elspeth.

'Help me up,' said Elspeth.

'Let's get you to the hospital fast,' said Hamish.

'It's all right,' said Elspeth. 'She didn't get me. I'm wearing one of the colonel's old flak jackets.'

Hamish rounded on Mr Johnson. 'Why was Elspeth left alone with this woman?'

'I told them to,' said Elspeth. 'I thought I would be safe.'

Perry came running out. 'What's happened?'

'Oh, Perry,' said Elspeth and burst into tears. He wrapped his arms around her.

'Hamish, the phones are back on,' said Mr Johnson.

'Right. Help me get her into the office and I'll get Jimmy ower from Strathbane.'

In the office with ex-policeman Clarry taking notes, Hamish switched on the small tape recorder he always carried with him and charged Tilly with attempted culpable homicide. She had subsided into a mutinous silence.

Hamish tried question after question but she just stared at him defiantly.

At last Hamish picked up the phone and, consulting his notebook, dialled Colin Framont's number. 'Colin, I have arrested your wife,' he said. 'Come up to the hotel.'

'No,' said Tilly. 'You have no right to bring him here.'

'I have every right.'

'Filth. You're all filth,' said Tilly.

'What, men?'

'Aye, the lot of you, and you will roast in hell for your bestial lusts.'

'Confession is good for the soul,' said Hamish. 'Why don't we begin at the beginning? Let's start with Catriona Beldame.'

'He went to her. My Colin. He'd never even disobeyed me before. He had to be stopped. Oh, she looked that startled when herself saw me, lying naked in her sinful bed. But I shut her up for good.'

'You could have been caught lighting that fuse,' said Hamish.

'Not me. The Lord was with me that day.'

'But Ina? Why Ina?'

A tear ran down one of her cheeks and she brushed it angrily away. 'She was my best friend. We were always agreed on everything.

Keep the men in their place and if they won't stay there, give them a good whack. I thought she'd be pleased but she said it was on her conscience and she felt she ought to tell the police. The Lord was watching over me again and he sent down a fog to cover me when I darted into Patel's and killed her.'

'And Ellie Macpherson?'

'I couldn't take a chance. She had to be silenced. The Lord told me she had to be silenced.'

'And Fiona McNulty?'

'That hoor. I made Colin tell me about her. He said Fergus had been seeing her. My Ina's husband betraying her by going to a whore.'

Jimmy Anderson came in flanked by Harry MacNab and a policewoman.

'I have her confessions on tape,' said Hamish wearily. 'You'll find Clarry has excellent shorthand notes as well. Take her away and interview her yourself, Jimmy.'

Hamish found Colin Framont in the hall. He turned his head away as Tilly was taken past him.

'You as well,' said Jimmy, taking Colin's arm. 'Hamish, file a full report.'

Colin was led out protesting that he knew nothing about it.

Hamish went back to where Priscilla was looking blankly at the stairs. 'Where's Elspeth?'

'She and Perry have gone to file a story. Want a drink?'

'Just the one. I never asked where Blair was.'

They went into the bar. Hamish was miserable because the murderer had turned out to be one of the villagers. Priscilla was miserable because Perry and Elspeth seemed to be close.

They ordered whiskies and sat in silence for a while. Then Priscilla said, 'You should have gone with them. You solved the case.'

'The old, old reason, Priscilla. Too much focus on me means a promotion and promotion means moving to Strathbane.'

'I can hardly believe it,' said Priscilla. 'I worked with Tilly from time to time on visits up here when there was a crofters' fair or something like that.'

'She beat her husband.' Hamish took a swallow of his whisky. 'Fergus's wife beat him, too, and I'm supposed to know everything that goes on in the village. I wonder what other bit of misery is going on behind closed doors that I don't know about. You seem pretty low. Get a fright?'

'Yes, something like that.'

When Hamish got back to the police station, he typed out a report and sent it over to Strathbane. Then he took the dog and cat out for a walk through the snow on the waterfront.

The loch was glassy black. The air was still and crisp and cold. Bright stars shone down overhead. A television set in one of the cottages was playing a comedy, and the sound of canned laughter made Hamish feel as if the old gods were laughing at him for being such a blind fool.

What was it Archie had said? 'We don't do sex in Lochdubh.'

Poor buggers, thought Hamish. He had a bright picture of Priscilla staring desolately at the stairs when Elspeth and Perry had just gone up to write their story.

'Poor me,' he said out loud.

Chapter Eleven

The weaker sex, to piety more prone.
– Sir William Alexander,
Earl of Stirling

Jimmy called the following morning. 'She's gone completely round the twist, Hamish.'

'Are you sure she's not just pretending to be mad to get out of a trial?'

'Blair finished her off, in a way. He insisted on doing the questioning while I sat there like a tumshie. Tilly decided he was the devil's messenger and she quoted the Bible at him nonstop. If you hadn't got that confession out o' her, he might have had a job proving her guilty. And would you get this? They dug up the garden and found a computer and a supply o' chemicals. More than that, our Tilly studied chemistry for a year at Strathbane University before dropping out. Blair's trying to take the credit but Daviot read your statement. I think he's going to promote you this time. Give you a policeman to help you.'

'Oh, no!'

'Relax. He's just putting you up to sergeant. He says this police station, as he remembers it, has two bedrooms.'

'Chust the one.'

'Come on, Hamish. You look shifty. Show it to me.'

'Oh, all right.' Hamish led him into the living room. He pulled back a curtain next to the bookcase, revealing a door. He opened it.

Jimmy looked in. 'What on earth . . .?'

'I chust used it over the years to put away stuff that might come in handy,' said Hamish.

'An old fridge, a broken electric kettle, a lawn mower, and that's just the stuff that's blocking the entrance. You'll need to get a skip and clean the place out.'

'I don't want a policeman living with me.'

'Settle for it, laddie. It's either that or Strathbane. I gather they're going ahead with Catriona's funeral this afternoon.'

'Yes. There was some fuss about her being buried in consecrated ground, but Rory McBride is having her cremated and taking the ashes away with him. There's a service in the kirk at three o'clock this afternoon and then what's left of her body will be taken to the crematorium at Strathbane.'

'Won't be many there, I suppose.'

'The women will turn up. They'll say it is their Christian duty but it's just an excuse to wear a hat and gossip. They fair frighten me now. I feel I don't really know what they're like.'

'Better not to. You know, Hamish, the day I discovered I didn't understand women at all was a great relief. After that, I just learned to take them as they came.'

'Unfortunate choice of words, Jimmy.'

'Got any whisky?'

'The sun isn't even over the yardarm.'

'This is still winter. The sun has barely the strength to crawl up the sky.'

'Oh, all right. Just the one. How's Colin taking it?'

'I think he'll be all right. I took him home late last night. Fergus came round and hugged him and said he'd stay the night.'

'Maybe they'll be able to help each other get over this.'

Hamish went up to the church in the afternoon. The Currie sisters had put in an appearance along with Mrs Wellington. Rory McBride was there. Other than that, the church was deserted. Mr Wellington gave a short sermon, they sang several hymns, and then the undertaker's men, who had been smoking outside the church, came in and bore off the coffin with the remains of Catriona.

Hamish gave a sigh of relief as the hearse drove off followed by one single car, driven by Rory McBride.

'I hope never to see another person like Catriona as long as I live,' he said.

'He's talking to himself again,' came the voice of Nessie Currie. 'Daft, that's what he is.'

Hamish made his escape.

Priscilla had decided to hold a small party for Elspeth and Perry, who were leaving the following morning. She wanted to somehow get a date with Perry even if it meant going to Glasgow to see him. She phoned the forensic lab and invited Lesley in the hope that Lesley would keep Hamish occupied. Mr Johnson was invited and Angela and Dr Brodie as well. She decided she'd better ask Matthew Campbell and his wife and maybe Mr and Mrs Wellington and the long-staying guest, Dominic Garry. Then she realized she hadn't told Hamish about the party. She phoned him and he said he would be there.

Priscilla was glad that her parents were away visiting friends in Caithness. Her father was quite capable of asking Perry to marry her.

* * *

Hamish was getting ready for the party when he heard someone knocking at the kitchen door. He had just finished shaving. He wrapped a towel around his neck and went to answer the door.

Lesley stood there, beaming. 'I thought I would drive you up to the party,' she said. 'That way you can drink as much as you like.'

'I never was much of a drinker,' said Hamish. 'And I'd like to take my own vehicle. I never know when I'll be called out.'

'Aren't you going to ask me in?'

'Just for a minute.'

Lesley swept past him in a cloud of perfume. She shrugged off her coat. She was wearing a transparent spangly white chiffon blouse. Hamish could clearly see that underneath it she was wearing a very sturdy white brassiere. A short scarlet skirt, sheer stockings and high heels completed the ensemble.

'I'm sorry I shut the door on you,' said Lesley. 'You see, when you turned up in your uniform and with your pets, I assumed you just didn't care.'

'Why should I care that much?' asked Hamish. 'It's not as if we're an item.'

'But we could be! You are to be promoted to sergeant but with my help, you could go a lot further.'

'Lesley, I really need to finish dressing. I do

not want to be helped to fame and glory. I will see you at the party.'

Lesley could not quite believe this was happening. She had built up such a romantic scene in her mind. As the only woman in the lab, she had turned down date after date until she had begun to think of herself as irresistible. She had taken Hamish's advice and warned them all that she would report anyone for sexual harassment who overstepped the mark. The rude jokes and nasty things in her locker had promptly ceased, to be replaced with romantic tributes like chocolates and flowers.

She did not know that her colleagues had opened a betting book to see who could seduce her first.

Hamish turned away. 'Shut the door on your way out.'

Priscilla and Elspeth had both spent a long time working on their appearances. As it was not a dressy affair and taking place early in the evening, Priscilla had settled for a classic look: soft blue cashmere sweater with a matching skirt and a sapphire-and-pearl choker necklace.

Elspeth, who had a limited wardrobe, had decided on the Edith Piaf look to match her frizzy hair. She had put on a short black dress and plenty of white foundation cream, white powder and scarlet lipstick.

They entered the lounge at the same time, covertly eyeing each other. Elspeth immediately felt like a freak. She got a glimpse of herself in a mirror and thought miserably that she looked ill rather than attractive.

She fled back upstairs and scrubbed off the white make-up and replaced it with something more subdued.

By the time she went back down, most of the guests had arrived, with the exception of Perry.

Angela Brodie went up to Hamish. 'You really do scrub up well,' she said.

Hamish was wearing a beautifully tailored charcoal-grey suit with a silk tie. He had found the suit in a charity shop and was amazed to find when he got it home that it fitted him perfectly.

'You're looking charming yourself,' said Hamish gallantly although Angela was wearing a droopy dress as grey as her wispy hair.

Perry entered and stood in the doorway of the lounge, smiling all around.

Priscilla and Elspeth went straight up to him and began to talk. Hamish scowled. 'What's up?' teased Angela. 'You don't want them but don't want anyone else to have them?'

Hamish scowled harder and moved away from her. He waited for an opportunity. Mrs Wellington went up to them and then drew

Priscilla away. Matthew Campbell approached them and began to talk.

Hamish went over to Perry. 'You haven't got a drink. Come with me to the bar.'

'I barely recognized you,' said Perry. 'You ought to dress up more often.' He said to the barman, 'I'll have a whisky.'

Perry was feeling warm and tipsy. Priscilla had sent a bottle of chilled champagne to his room earlier with the compliments of the hotel, and somehow he had drunk the lot.

'Don't you ever get bored up here, Hamish?' he asked.

'Och, no, there is always something funny going on.' Hamish began to tell Perry some highly amusing and completely fictitious highland stories. From time to time either Elspeth or Priscilla tried to butt in, but Perry blocked them out as Hamish's soft highland voice went on and on.

The party began to thin out. Lesley cast one anguished look at Hamish and then left. Hamish saw her leave out of the corner of one eye, gave her ten minutes, and then said, 'Grand talking to you. Got to go.'

'But . . .' began Perry. Hamish was already rapidly making his way out of the lounge.

Priscilla was caught up, saying goodbye to various guests. Then she found Elspeth beside her. 'Perry has left,' she whispered.

'Where has he gone?'

'Mr Johnson said he went upstairs and put on his coat and went out. He said he shouldn't be driving after the amount he's drunk. He said he seemed tipsy.'

'Hamish!' said Priscilla. 'Hamish has charmed the boots off him. I bet he's gone down to the station.'

'Let's go down there,' said Elspeth, she and Priscilla being joined in sisterly fury at Hamish. 'We could listen outside and see if Perry talks about us.'

Hamish had just taken off his tie and jacket when he heard a knock at the kitchen door. 'If that's you, Lesley,' he shouted, 'I've gone to bed.'

'No, it's me, Perry.'

Hamish opened the door. 'Come in. I'll get the coffee on. You should never have driven after all you've had to drink. What's up?'

'You just left. I thought maybe we could continue our conversation.'

'I'm afraid not. I'm right tired and want to go to bed.'

'Good idea,' said Perry softly.

I must be mistaken, thought Hamish, plugging in the percolator. 'Take your coat off. Coffee won't be long.'

Perry had driven so slowly and carefully

that Elspeth and Priscilla had not been long behind him.

They were now crouched in the snow outside the kitchen window.

'Do you know, you've got the most marvellously long eyelashes,' said Perry.

Hamish sighed. 'I think a mistake is being made here, laddie. Just to make things plain: I am heterosexual.'

'But you were chatting me up!' cried Perry.

'I told you a lot of stories but not once did I say anything at all that would lead you to think I fancied you, now did I?'

'I thought . . .'

'You've had a lot to drink. Forget the coffee. I'm taking you back to the hotel right now. You can get someone to come down in the morning to collect your car.'

Outside, shivering in the snow, Elspeth and Priscilla stared at each other.

'I'm cold,' said Elspeth. 'Let's go inside and have some of that coffee.'

They crunched through the frozen snow. Hamish had left the door unlocked. They both went in and sat at the kitchen table and stared gloomily at each other.

'I'm slipping,' said Elspeth. 'I never for a moment suspected a thing.'

'Nor me,' said Priscilla. 'Hamish must have been trying to protect us.'

Elspeth snorted. 'Not that one. He deliberately took up all Perry's attention out of sheer jealousy. I'll get the coffee.'

'If he did that, I would like revenge,' said Priscilla. 'What about sending Lesley some flowers and saying they're from him.'

'No, she'd just get hurt, and from the way she kept looking over at Hamish, he'd hurt her already. I don't see his pets.'

'He's probably taken his wives with him,' said Priscilla. 'His damn animals come first.'

Hamish, driving back to the police station, spotted Elspeth's car parked a little way away along the waterfront. He stopped his own vehicle and went quietly towards the police station. He heard their voices from the kitchen. He walked back to his Land Rover and drove back to the hotel.

Mr Johnson reluctantly said he could have a room for the night, but the dog and cat would have to stay in the kitchen.

Hamish waited an hour and then crept downstairs. The night porter was, as usual, asleep with his feet up on the desk. He went into the kitchen and summoned Sonsie and Lugs, who followed him quietly upstairs to his room. He hoped he would not run into Perry.

By the time Priscilla found out in the morning that Hamish had stayed the night at the hotel he had already left.

Elspeth and Perry departed the next day, and a few hours later Priscilla left as well. No one wanted to say goodbye to Hamish Macbeth.

More snow roared down from the north in the afternoon. Hamish found the sudden lack of activity made him feel restless. Usually he welcomed a chance to return to his old ways of sloping around the village or taking long drives over his extensive beat. He tried to phone Priscilla but was told that she had left.

Then there was another power cut and the phones also went dead. Hamish would often say that he never watched very much television but he found that with the snow preventing him from going anywhere, he missed it badly.

He spent the day performing his usual chores as best as he could and tidying up the old files in the filing cabinet and promising himself that as soon as the power came back on he would transfer them on to his computer.

At last, unable to bear the inactivity any longer, he put on his snowshoes and, bending before the torrent of horizontal snow, fought his way along to see Angela Brodie.

As he approached, he heard the thud of a

generator and saw that the lights were on in the doctor's cottage.

Angela welcomed him and asked to hear all about how he had solved the murders, saying that she had not had an opportunity to ask him at the party because Hamish had spent all his time with Perry.

Hamish winced inside. If it had not been for his regrettable streak of highland malice he would at least have had the pleasure of looking forward to seeing Priscilla again.

Hamish accepted a glass of whisky, checking it carefully for cat hairs before he drank any. As he talked about the murders, he reflected how strange and distant it all seemed already.

When he had finished, Angela said, 'I hope that good-looking journalist, Perry, is not out to make trouble.'

'Why?'

'He came to see me yesterday. I gather he was interested on doing a piece on the lack of sex in Lochdubh.'

'I hope not. That would distress a lot of people.'

'Last week Mrs Halburton-Smythe met me at Patel's. She seemed to have high hopes of Priscilla marrying Perry.'

'Perry's gay.'

'Is he now? Pity. These good-looking men who take care of their appearance often are.

Oh, two men were seen up on the mountains yesterday.'

'I hope they're all right,' said Hamish. 'The Highlands are plagued with amateur climbers. They have road signs for deer crossing, schools, elderly people crossing and all that. They should have a warning sign showing a falling climber. In Glencoe in the winter, it fair rains falling climbers. I wish the snow would ease up. I havenae been to see old Angus for a while.'

'I got the weather report on my computer. Rain is supposed to be coming in from the west tonight.'

'That'll mean flooding in other parts. We've been pretty lucky in Lochdubh.'

'Not thinking about getting married?'

'Who to?' demanded Hamish. 'Elspeth was mooning over that Perry and so was Priscilla.'

'What about that girl Lesley?'

'Oh, her. She wanted to make me over.'

'Never mind, Hamish. You should travel more. Maybe meet a nice girl.'

'Angela, I went to Spain, mind? And I was stuck in an hotel wi' a bundle o' geriatrics. I've never been so popular wi' the opposite sex in my life.'

'You can't write off foreign travel just because of one unlucky holiday.'

'I'll see. Thanks for the whisky.'

When Hamish left, the snow was still falling but it had a dampish sleety feel. He made supper for himself and his pets, cooking on top of the stove by gaslight and then, carrying a lamp into the bedroom, undressed and got into bed. He read a detective story until his eyes began to droop, so he turned out the gas lamp and went to sleep.

He was awakened in the morning by a loud thump as melting snow fell off the roof.

Hamish got dressed and went outside. The wind had shifted around to the west and was blowing mild air in from the Gulf Stream. Everything glittered in the morning sun and the air was full of the sound of running water.

He got a shovel out of the shed and began to clear a path from the kitchen door. By midday the electricity had come on again and the phone was operating.

In the afternoon he called in at Patel's, bought a bag of groceries, and headed up the hill to Angus Macdonald's cottage.

'I knew you would call today,' said Angus, graciously accepting the provisions.

'Saw it in your crystal ball, did you?' asked Hamish.

'Sit down. I'll just be putting this stuff away.'

'Any chance of a coffee?'

'Aye.'

Hamish sat by the smouldering peat fire. Angus had not bothered to go through his usual performance of hanging the blackened kettle over the fire to boil. That was all part of his act as an Olden Tymes seer, and he couldn't be bothered wasting it on Hamish.

Angus came back from the kitchen and handed Hamish a mug of coffee. Hamish took a sip and made a face. 'This is dreadful stuff, Angus.'

'Is it now. It was yourself who gave me a jar of that last year.'

'I remember,' said Hamish. 'It was one of Patel's special offers. I came to see how you were doing, Angus, but you seem to be fine.'

'I'm all right but it iss yourself you ought to be worrying about.'

'Why?'

'There were these two men seen up on the mountain yesterday.'

'Angela told me about them. Climbers.'

'I closed my eyes,' crooned Angus, 'and I saw evil.'

Hamish knew that Angus had a very powerful telescope.

'What did you see?' he demanded.

'I saw they were carrying rifles. No climbing equipment.'

Hamish thought of the two escaped poachers.

'Well, they wouldn't hang around up there in the blizzard,' he said. 'Or with any luck, they've frozen to death.'

'Have a look in the bothy up the brae,' said Angus.

Hamish returned to the police station and collected a powerful torch, told his pets to stay where they were, and set off up the brae at the back and then to the lower slopes of the Two Sisters, the twin mountains that dominated Lochdubh.

The bothy, a shepherd's hut, was at the top of a slope. Hamish struggled up through the soft melting snow, feeling his feet and trousers beginning to get wet.

He opened the door of the bothy and went in. There was a pan on the battered old stove in the corner with a few baked beans at the bottom. He shone the torch on the earthen floor, puddled with melting snow seeping into the ramshackle hut. There was a boot print in one corner and in another, a few empty cans.

His heart sank. He was sure somehow it was the poachers. Climbers usually tidied up after themselves.

He went outside and phoned Jimmy. 'I think those poachers are back,' said Hamish. 'They've been spotted up the back of Lochdubh. It's dark now but I think if you send a squad over, we could get started first light.'

'Wait a minute. I'll see what I can do.'

Hamish waited and waited. At last Jimmy came back on the line. 'Can't do anything, Hamish. There's a big drug bust tomorrow and Blair says he needs all the men he can get.'

'But these men are armed!'

'All I can suggest is that you keep close to your station and don't try to go after them yourself. Look, as soon as this drug business is over, I'll come myself with as many men as I can get.'

The next day Hamish was determined not to let fear of the poachers trap him in his police station. Just in case they came calling at the station, he left the dog and cat with Angela, explaining that he did not want to return home and find them shot.

He debated whether to round up some of the local men to help him in the search but decided against it. If one of them got shot in the hunt, he would never forgive himself. He had phoned Jimmy again, who had said Blair still refused to send any men. With his deer rifle beside him, he set out, driving up and over the hills, stopping occasionally at croft houses to ask if anyone had seen the two men.

The weather was mild with the first hint of spring, and the snow was melting rapidly. Burns were in full spate, tumbling down the hillsides, their peaty gold water flashing in the sun.

He searched bothies and outhouses for any sign of where they might have spent the night. The bothy he was sure they had been staying in was deserted. He was glad when night fell, feeling always that the scope of a rifle held by someone up on the hills was trained on him.

Hamish phoned Jimmy and asked him to send over photographs of the two men. When they arrived, he printed copies of them and went out and stuck them up on the lampposts along the waterfront.

That evening he carried an armchair from his living room and set it against the kitchen door. Then he slept in it, fully dressed, with his rifle at his side. He awoke briefly during the night, feeling pins and needles in his legs.

By morning he felt dirty and gritty and he was in a foul mood. It was more than likely that the poachers were not after him but simply hiding out from the police.

Nonetheless, he went out searching again, without success. The sun was warm; it was as if the blizzards had never happened and all the misery that Catriona had brought to the village was rapidly disappearing in the clear light.

When he went back to the village and was making his way to Angela's house to pick up his animals again he saw a rare sight. Archie

Maclean and his wife were walking hand in hand along the waterfront. Other couples were strolling along either holding hands as well or with their arms around each other's waists.

'What's happening?' Hamish asked Angela when she answered the door to him. 'Has romance come to Lochdubh or is there another witch around selling love potions?'

'It's pretty awful. Haven't you seen the newspaper? It's that cursed Perry.'

Hamish followed her into the kitchen. She handed him a newspaper folded over at a feature and said, 'Read that.'

The headline was enough for Hamish. WE DON'T DO SEX IN LOCHDUBH. Underneath was a smaller headline: WAS IT FRUSTRATED SEX THAT CAUSED THE LOCHDUBH MURDERS?

Hamish ran his eyes over the piece. It mentioned the fact that even the village constable was celibate.

The Currie sisters were quoted as saying, 'We don't go in for any nastiness like that round here.'

Hamish checked the other quotes, and his eyes narrowed. 'There's a lot wrong here, Angela. I have a feeling that he asked the Currie sisters, for example, if they went in for S and M in the village. He put down replies but omitted the questions.'

Hamish phoned Elspeth. When she came on the line, he said, 'Thon was a malicious piece of writing from Perry.'

'Maybe it was because he was disappointed in love,' said Elspeth. 'Fancied you, didn't he?'

'Cut that out. Do you know if he taped those interviews?'

'He taped everything. He doesn't know any shorthand.'

'Can you get me the tape?'

'He'd know it was me if I took it.'

'Do you think he ever leaves it in his car?'

'I think he keeps it in the glove compartment when he's not working.'

'So break into his car and pinch it. Pinch the car if necessary.'

'Why should I?'

Hamish took a deep breath. 'This is a rotten malicious piece of reporting and you know it. Do you want someone like that on the staff?'

There was a long silence and then Elspeth said reluctantly, 'I'll see what I can do.'

Elspeth flicked through a notebook she kept in her desk with the names of various villains. Sonny Turner had recently finished doing time for stealing cars. She made a note of his address and after work made her way to an address in Clydebank.

Sonny recognized her as a reporter he had seen on the press benches in the high court and tried to close the door.

Elspeth put her foot in the door and held up a fifty-pound note. 'I'm writing an article on car theft. I know you're clean but I want a bit of advice.'

He nipped the note from her fingers and then opened the door wide.

'Come in, petal,' he said. 'You've come tae the right man.'

Elspeth knew that Perry lived in a cul-de-sac off Great Western Road. She drove there at four in the morning. Perry's BMW was parked on the road outside.

She crouched down by the car and assembled her kit – a wooden door wedge, a metal wire coat hanger and a hammer.

Following Sonny's instructions, she broke into the car. The alarm shrilled. With a beating heart she dived into the car and, as per instructions, locked the door, unlocked it, opened the door from the inside, and hit the kill switch on the underside of the dashboard.

The alarm fell silent. She peered up at the windows. Not a single light showed. People were used to faulty car alarms. She opened the glove compartment and seized Perry's small tape recorder. Then to make it look like a real burglary, she took his radio and CD player as well.

She let herself out of the car, stuffed the stolen goods and her equipment back into a travel bag, and scurried off to where she had parked her own car.

Back in her own apartment, she switched on the tape recorder and ran it back to the Lochdubh interviews. It was as Hamish had expected. The Currie sisters were asked whether the women of the village liked to dress up as fantasy figures, nurses or little girls, to excite their husbands.

Mrs Wellington had been asked if she ever wore leather in bed or had used a vibrator.

'The sexual practises you are talking about are filth,' Mrs Wellington had said.

But her reply as published in the article had appeared as, 'All sex is filth.'

The other interviews were on the same tricky lines. Various villagers had been asked about Hamish's love life and the replies had been mostly the same – that he did not have a girlfriend at the moment. Nothing about him being celibate.

Elspeth felt the fury rise in her. Poor innocent Lochdubh, held up to ridicule.

Wearing the thin gloves she had donned for the burglary, she typed out a note to the news desk at Scottish Television and packed up the tape recorder and the original article.

She addressed the package and then drove to Scottish Television wearing an old motorcycle helmet and leathers from the days when she had used a motorbike. She studied herself in the mirror. Nobody could tell in her disguise whether she was a man or a woman.

Elspeth was sent to cover the high court the next day. A case of drug pushing dragged on and then was finally adjourned to the following day.

By the time she got back to the office, it was buzzing with the news of Perry's sacking. Scottish Television had played the tape on the lunchtime news.

A troubleshooter had been sent to Lochdubh to pacify the maligned villagers with money.

Perry had tried to blame Elspeth and was told roundly to forget it. He had made enough trouble already. Elspeth heaved a sigh of relief. She still had the stolen radio and CD player in her flat.

The newspaper published a full apology. The villagers were compensated. Hamish found himself the pleased beneficiary of one thousand pounds. As soon as it had arisen, the public demonstration of affection disappeared and Lochdubh settled into its old ways.

Chapter Twelve

To travel hopefully is a better thing than to arrive.

– Robert Louis Stevenson

Lochdubh settled down into its usual placid ways. Hamish hoped the poachers were long gone.

He opened the door one misty morning to find his mother standing on the step. He stooped down and gave her a hug. 'What brings you?'

'I've a rare treat for you, Hamish,' said Mrs Macbeth, sitting at the table and opening up a capacious leather handbag. 'Have you heard o' Pedro's Olive Oil?'

Hamish shook his red head. 'And what did you win this time?' he asked. His mother was addicted to entering competitions.

'This!' She pulled out a folder. 'It's a four-day trip to Barcelona, first class on Eurostar to Paris, then Grande Classe on a train called the

Joan Miró and a few nights in a hotel. You'd need to leave in two weeks' time.'

'Can't you give it to anyone else, Mum? I mean, I've been to Spain.'

'It's a great big country. You've got to get out a bit.'

'How did you win?'

'I wrote a slogan, "Pedro's health-giving olive oil can give you long life." See! Simple. Better to keep it simple. They've got a photo o' a fellow who looks like a Spanish Father Christmas to put on the bottles.'

'And that's it? What if someone uses the stuff aged thirty and drops dead?'

'I don't have to bother about that. Anyway, it's all in the words. I said "can", not "will".' A note of steel entered her voice. 'What you need is a holiday. I'm leaving this folder here and in a fortnight's time, I want to hear you're on your way.'

In vain did Hamish protest. His mother slapped the folder down on the table and left.

Two days later, feeling he had done his duty by driving the many miles over his beat, he decided to take himself up into the hills. A little part of him was still worried that the poachers were out to get him.

It was a grand day as he headed up into the mountains. The peaks of the Two Sisters were still covered in snow. The days were getting longer already, which was cheering. There was so very little daylight in the north in winter.

A curlew piped its mournful note and up above, a golden eagle flashed its wings in the sun. He turned and looked back at the village. He could see a figure that looked like Archie Maclean painting something on a board outside his cottage. He took out a small pair of powerful binoculars and focussed on the notice. It said, TRIPS ROUND THE BAY IN A GENUINE SCOTTISH FISHING BOAT.

Hamish remembered that Archie had decided to try his hand in a bit of tourism when the summer came along. The fish stocks were dwindling, and he had been searching around for a way to make some extra money.

Right down the hill something glinted in the heather.

Hamish took to his heels and ran. He looked briefly back over his shoulder. Two men with guns had risen out of the heather where they had been hiding.

Hamish was a champion hill runner. He ran like the wind heading up and up to a particular plateau he knew. The round tarns, those ponds like miniature Scottish lochs left behind by the Ice Age, shone like so many giants' blue eyes in the sun.

On and on ran Hamish until he gained the plateau, which was covered by a peat bog.

Experienced in the treacheries of the bog, he leapt from tussock to tussock, gained the far side, and crouched down behind a large boulder.

He was unarmed. He took out his mobile phone and found that the battery was dead.

His wits against two rifles! He could only hope it would work.

What were their names again? Ah, he had it. The older one was Walter Wills and the younger, Granger Home.

He cautiously looked round the rock in time to see the two men on the far side of the bog.

'There's the bastard!' shouted Wally. He raised his rifle. Hamish withdrew his head as a bullet pinged off the rock.

Sound carried in the clear air. He heard Wally saying, 'He cannae be armed or he'd ha' shot back. Come on. Let's get him.'

Down below at his cottage window, Angus the seer put down his powerful telescope and hurtled out of his cottage and down the brae to the village, crying for help.

'Come on, come on,' muttered Hamish.

Suddenly there was a cry. 'Get me out o' here!'

Hamish peered round the rock. Granger had

fallen into a peat bog. Wally put his gun down on the heather and tried to pull him out. 'I'm sinking,' moaned Granger. 'You've got to hold me.'

'Here!' said Wally. 'Hold on tae the butt o' my rifle and I'll pull you out.'

There was a loud shot and Wally fell to the ground.

He forgot to put the safety catch on, thought Hamish. The man's shot himself.

Hamish hurried towards them. Someone had left a long branch, which they had been using as a walking stick. He seized it and then crouched down by Granger. 'I'm going to wedge this under your arms. Don't move or struggle. I'll get help.'

He then went to Wally. The man's blank eyes looked up to the indifferent sky.

'I shot him.' Tears ran down Granger's cheeks. 'When I grabbed his rifle, I must ha' pulled the trigger.'

'I won't be long,' said Hamish.

He ran off. Further down the slope he met a posse of ghillies and gamekeepers and told them what had happened.

'Air-sea rescue'll be along in a minute. They can pull him out of the bog,' said one ghillie.

By the time they returned, a helicopter had come over the mountains and was hovering over the bog. Two men came down. 'The best thing you can do,' said Hamish, 'is get a rope round him and pull him out.'

As they fastened the rope under Graham's armpits, Hamish charged him with attempted murder.

The rope was then tied securely on to the cable, and the helicopter was signalled to haul away.

The rope strained, and then, with a great plop like a cork being pulled out of a bottle, Granger was up and out of the bog.

'Get a stretcher down and lash him on to it,' ordered Hamish.

'There's no need for that at all,' said an ambulance man. 'The winch is here. They can haul both of us up.'

'I'm ordering you to get this man on a stretcher. I fear he may attack you.'

'I'm a paramedic and he looks as quiet as a lamb to me. Come on, son, let's get you winched up.'

Hamish watched as the two figures rose up to the helicopter. Then the paramedic screamed and Granger fell, spiralling straight down. He smashed into the rock Hamish had been hiding behind and lay still.

Sirens were sounding in the village below.

Another paramedic was winched down. His face was white with shock. 'He knifed Johnny.'

'Is Johnny going to be all right?' asked Hamish.

'Aye, he just slashed at his hand. Is this fellow dead?'

'Yes, very. I think he blamed himself for the death of his friend. I was worried something like this might happen.'

It was to be a long day. The bodies of Walter and Granger were winched up to be taken to the procurator fiscal in Strathbane.

Hamish told the ghillies and keepers to make sure none of the approaching police went into the bog.

Jimmy Anderson eventually arrived, gasping and panting, surrounded by armed police.

'You're too late,' said Hamish. 'Two dead men. Where's Blair?'

'Down in his car. You won't see him climbing up anywhere.'

Hamish described what had happened. 'Lot of paperwork for you,' said Jimmy when Hamish had finished. 'You weren't armed?'

'No.'

'That's a mercy. I wouldn't put it past Blair to try to claim you shot Wally.'

'Do you want me to help you down the hill?'

'Hamish, I've got to stay here for the forensic team. You'd better go down and report to Blair. Have you heard the news about Lesley?'

'No. What?'

'She's engaged to be married to her boss, Bruce. She did ask me to be sure to let you know.'

'I'm not going down to report to Blair,' said Hamish. 'Tell him I'm looking for clues or something.'

Jimmy's phone rang. Hamish, listening, assumed it was Blair. He wandered off up the hillside until the scene below him grew smaller and smaller. He stayed up in the mountains until dark when he returned to the police station and wearily began to type up his report.

Epilogue

He seldom errs
Who thinks the worst he can of womankind.
– John Home

Hamish had decided to take his mother's offer of a free holiday. His first duty was to call at the London office of Pedro's Olive Oil to be photographed and given the large bouquet of flowers that had originally been intended for his mother.

Hamish made two speeches extolling the virtues of the oil, shook hands all round, allowed himself to be embraced several times, and then was sent on his way with a gift of one thousand euros and his train tickets.

The ceremony being over, he travelled to St Pancras station to catch the Eurostar.

He did not know that his first-class ticket allowed him a special entrance to avoid the rush or that there was a lounge for first-class passengers, so he waited in the vast and highly uncomfortable general waiting room. There were horseshoe sofa arrangements in front of round tables, which, by the geographical siting of chairs and tables, meant that only two people could make use of the table. Other rows of seats were backless. There was only one small café and one small newsagent to service all the hordes.

When the train departure was announced everyone rushed to the escalators, fretting and fidgeting while passports and tickets were checked.

At last he was on board. What maniac had designed the seating? he wondered.

He was seated at a table, one passenger beside him and two across. There was very little legroom. He put his long legs out into the corridor but kept having to draw them in when people came past. The man opposite him was nearly as tall as Hamish and so they worked out that Hamish should stretch his feet out to the left and his fellow traveller to the right.

During the two-and-a-half-hour journey, they were served three-course meals with wine. Hamish's opposite companion had a burning desire to go to the loo as soon as the food was served. In trying to stand up and get over Hamish's legs, he stumbled, held on to his tray for support, stumbled against Hamish, and knocked Hamish's meal across into the lap of the woman opposite.

What screams and swear words until the woman was cleaned down and presented with a complimentary bottle of champagne. No one suggested replacing Hamish's dinner, and he was too fed up by this time to demand one.

He finally got out in Paris at the Gare du Nord. Rain was thudding down on the roof. Outside a line of people waiting for taxis seemed to stretch for miles. He pulled a thin raincoat out of his backpack, put it on, and began to trudge through the streets of Paris. He knew the next train left from the Gare d'Austerlitz on the Left Bank of the Seine.

He dropped into various brasseries for comforting hot drinks, then he would consult his map and plough on.

At Bastille, he saw a cruising cab and flagged it down. The rain had thinned and watery sunlight was gilding the greenish brown waters of the Seine as the taxi crossed the river and then swung into the courtyard of the Gare d'Austerlitz.

The train, the Joan Miró, was already standing on the platform. The coach attendant took away his ticket and passport and said he would return them before arrival in Barcelona.

Hamish was ushered into his compartment. It contained a comfortable armchair and a private shower and toilet.

'Go straight to the dining car,' said the coach attendant. 'It gets very busy. Your bed will be made down when you return.'

Hamish began to enjoy himself for the first time. There was something pleasingly decadent at sitting at a dining table being served delicious food and wine while the lights of Paris whirled away in the distance.

When he returned to his cabin, he found a snowy white berth ready for him with a complimentary bar of chocolate on the pillow. Exploration of toilet and shower room revealed piles of fluffy towels and a bag with everything the traveller could need from a razor to soap and face flannel.

Hamish undressed and had a shower and then went to bed and fell fast asleep.

In the morning, he showered again, deciding that such a novelty should be tried twice, then dressed and went to the dining car, redolent with the sweet smell of croissant.

The first thing he decided after leaving the train was to leave his bag at the hotel in the Ramblas and walk down to the old port.

But waiting for him at the hotel was a smartly dressed executive from the olive oil company. After he had left his bag, he was whipped off to the factory on the outskirts, introduced to various directors, and taken on a tour of the bottling factory. Then there was a long lunch.

In the afternoon he was taken to the main factory to watch the refinery process. His guides were thorough. Then there was dinner with the executives and by the time he was taken back to his hotel, he was too weary to do anything else other than go to bed.

The same executive was waiting to trap him in the morning. This time it was out of Barcelona to the olive groves, wandering along rows of trees in the dusty heat. After lunch, more groves and then back to the city to the advertising office to study the layouts for the new labels.

Here he was praised for his slogan and asked to write a description of Pedro's Olive Oil.

'A bottle of golden sunshine to give you long life,' wrote Hamish and they all clapped as what he had written was translated.

Back to the factory where he was presented with a small silver cup and a crate of olive oil. They promised to send the olive oil on to him.

As he was now considered one of the team, the next long day involved talks on marketing and distribution. Hamish was aware that by tomorrow he had only one free day left. Where were the *señoritas* he had hoped to meet?

But to his relief, as the end of another long

and official dinner, he learned that next day he was to be left to his own devices.

The sun was shining brightly on the following morning. He walked down the Ramblas, that famous promenade, admiring the multitude of living statues, before ambling along the port and stopping at an outdoor fish restaurant for lunch. He was amused to see ashtrays on all the tables. France and Britain might sheepishly follow EU rules banning smoking but the Catalans did as they pleased.

He spent the afternoon back in the town buying various presents. He returned to the hotel, showered and changed into his best suit, and went up one of the side lanes off the Ramblas to a restaurant he had noticed earlier.

At the front, it looked as if it was just a small bar, but through the bar and to the side was a large restaurant.

It was full of young people and a good few thirty-somethings like himself. He ordered fish soup followed by a steak – he felt he had eaten enough paella to last him a lifetime, that seemingly being the favourite dish of the olive company.

There were two pretty girls at the next table. One leaned over to him. 'Are you English?'

'Scottish,' said Hamish.

'I'm Gerda from Germany – Berlin – and this

is Michelle from Paris. What brings you to Barcelona?'

Hamish told them all about the olive oil competition and about how he thought he would never get free of the factory. They laughed and laughed and then Hamish invited them to join him for coffee and brandy.

'It is good for Gerda to laugh,' said Michelle. 'She had a long relationship with a man and he left her for a woman old enough to be his mother. We are going on to a party tonight. Would you like come?'

'I'd love . . .' Hamish was just beginning when two middle-aged women bore down on them.

'It is!' one cried. 'It's Mr Macbeth. We were looking in the window and I said to Doris – that's Mr Macbeth. We'll never forget our time with you in Spain. So romantic! We need a favour. Could you walk us back to our hotel? We're nervous walking in the Ramblas at night.'

Hamish was dismally aware of the look of disgust Gerda was giving him and how Michelle was holding Gerda's hand and gazing sympathetically at her.

'I'll be back in a minute,' he said. 'Don't leave without me.'

He marched them sulkily to their hotel, refused offers of a drink, and as soon as they were indoors raced back to the restaurant.

But Gerda and Michelle were gone and had not even left a message for him.

Hamish haunted the restaurant at lunchtime next day, but there was no sign of them. He took in another couple of tourist sights and then packed and walked along to the station. This time the train was not the Joan Miró but an older, longer one. Once more he left his bag in the sleeping compartment and made his way to the restaurant car.

He was just finishing his main course of roast rabbit when the waiter asked if he would mind if a lady joined him. All the other places were taken up.

A woman sat down opposite him and said, 'Thanks.'

He guessed she was about his own age. She had thick dark hair, a long nose and a full red mouth. She held out her hand. 'I'm Caroline Evans.'

'Hamish Macbeth.'

'Scottish?'

'Aye.'

'I'm Welsh. Were you on holiday?'

'Not exactly.' Hamish gave her a gloomy report of his visit, and she laughed and laughed.

'It really is very funny, you know,' she said.

'You were hoping for sun, sex and sangria, I'll bet.'

'Something like that.'

'Tell me about yourself.'

Caroline began to talk about her work in Cardiff, which was running a cleaning agency, while Hamish relaxed and listened to the charming Welsh lilt of her voice.

He in turn told her about his work as a policeman in the north of Scotland and all about the recent murders while the dining car gradually emptied.

At last, he said, 'I think we should be leaving. Which is your compartment?'

'Number five.'

'There's a coincidence. Mine is number six.'

He walked her back along the corridor. He wanted to kiss her but thought that might be a bit too much since he had just met her. He said goodnight, went into his compartment and sat on the bed.

There was a knock at his door ten minutes later just as he was considering having a shower. He opened the door.

Caroline stood there in nightgown and negligee.

'I came to borrow a cup of sugar,' she said.

Hamish smiled down at her. 'You've come to the right place. Come on in!'

* * *

Detective Chief Inspector Blair sulkily followed his wife, Mary, into the delicatessen. Mary had said olive oil was healthier for cooking.

Blair suddenly felt he was being haunted. The artist in Barcelona had decided to put Hamish's picture on all the new bottles. From row after row of bottles, Hamish's face grinned down.

Blair turned about and went into the nearest pub. He had stopped drinking for five days and he was getting hallucinations. Must be the lack of alcohol.

He ordered a double whisky and then hid in a dark corner of the pub, hoping his wife would not find him.

If you enjoyed *Death of a Witch*, read on for the first chapter of the next book in the *Hamish Macbeth* series . . .

DEATH of a VALENTINE

Prologue

Over the heathery flanks of the mountains, over the lochs, over the vast tracts of land that make up the county of Sutherland in the very north of Scotland, down to the fishing boats bobbing at anchor along the west coast, the amazing news spread.

That most famous of highland bachelors, Police Sergeant Hamish Macbeth, was to be married at last. No, nothing like that mistake he had made before when he had nearly married some Russian. This was love. And he was to be married, right and proper, with a white wedding in the church in his home village of Lochdubh.

He was to marry his constable, Josie McSween, who had helped him solve the Valentine's Day murder. Pretty little thing she was with glossy brown hair and big brown eyes. The whole village of Lochdubh adored Josie. And everyone could see she was in love with Hamish.

On the great day, the church was full to bursting. Some wondered if the former love of Hamish's life, Priscilla Halburton-Smythe, would attend, but others whispered she was in Australia.

The added excitement was that Elspeth Grant, former reporter and now a star television news presenter, had promised to attend. She had many fans, and some had brought along their autograph books.

Josie's father was dead and she appeared not to have any male relatives. She was to be given away by Police Superintendent Peter Daviot.

There was a rustle of excitement as the bride arrived. Hamish stood erect at the altar, flanked by his best man, Detective Sergeant Jimmy Anderson. 'Cheer up!' muttered Jimmy. 'Man, you're as white as a sheet.'

The service began. Then at one point, the minister, Mr Wellington, addressed the congregation. 'If any amongst you know of any reason why this man and this woman should not be joined in holy matrimony, speak now, or forever hold your peace.' His deep highland voice held a note of amusement. For who could protest at such a love match?

Hamish Macbeth raised his eyes to the old beams on the church roof and murmured desperately the soldier's prayer.

'Dear God, if there is a God, get me out of this!'

Chapter One

It's hardly in a body's pow'r.
Tae keep, at times, frae being sour.
– Robert Burns

A year earlier

Hamish Macbeth had been promoted to sergeant. Having been promoted before and then reduced to the ranks, he had not even had to sit the necessary exams. Many a constable would have welcomed the promotion and the extra money that came with it, but Hamish was dismayed for two reasons. He was not an ambitious man and saw every rise up the ranks as a move to get him transferred to the city of Strathbane. All he wanted was to be left peacefully alone in his village police station.

He was also dismayed by being told that a constable would be coming to work with him and to clear out his spare room. The spare room was very highland in that it was stuffed with all sorts of rusting odds and ends that Hamish had picked up from time to time and had stored in the happy thought that they might come in useful one day.

At first he was confident that no one would want the job, but then he was told to expect a police constable, McSween.

He received a visit from his friend Detective Sergeant Jimmy Anderson. Jimmy walked in without knocking and found Hamish gloomily studying the contents of the spare room.

'For heaven's sakes, man,' exclaimed Jimmy. 'Get a move on. The lassie'll be here any minute.'

Hamish Macbeth, all six feet and five inches of him, turned slowly round. 'What lassie?'

'Your new copper. Wee Josie McSween.'

Hamish's hazel eyes looked blank with shock. 'Nobody told me it was a woman.'

'I overheard that curse o' your life, Blair, telling Daviot that the influence of a good woman was just what you need.'

Detective Chief Inspector Blair loathed Hamish and was always looking for ways to upset him.

'Come into the kitchen,' said Hamish. 'She cannae be staying here.'

'Why not? Got any whisky?'

'Usual place. Help yourself. No, she'll need to find lodgings.'

'It's the twenty-first century, Hamish. Nobody'll think anything of it.'

Jimmy sat down at the kitchen table and poured himself a drink. He was a smaller man than Hamish, with sandy hair and blue eyes in a foxy face.

'The twenty-first century has not arrived in Lochdubh,' said Hamish. 'Chust you sit there and enjoy your drink. I've got calls to make.'

Jimmy smiled and lay back in his chair. Although the month was April, a blizzard was blowing outside, 'the lambing blizzard' as the crofters bitterly called it, that storm which always seemed to hit the Highlands just after the lambs were born. The woodstove glowed with heat. Hamish's dog, Lugs, snored in a corner and his wild cat, Sonsie, lay over Jimmy's feet. He could hear Hamish making urgent phone calls from the police office but could not hear what he was saying.

At last, Hamish came back into the kitchen, looking cheerful. 'That's settled,' he said. 'All the women from the minister's wife down to the Currie sisters are phoning up headquarters to complain. Mrs Wellington has a spare room at the manse, and that's where she's going.'

'Josie's quite a tasty wee thing,' said Jimmy. 'What an old-fashioned dump this place is!'

'Better than that sink of a place, Strathbane,'

said Hamish. 'It's snowing like hell. The road'll be blocked.'

But in the fickle way of April blizzards, the snow abruptly stopped, the dark clouds rolled up the mountains, and soon a hot spring sun was rapidly melting the snow.

Josie set out, her heart beating with excitement. She was fairly small for a policewoman. She had masses of glossy brown hair and wide brown eyes. Her figure was a little on the plump side. Josie had fallen in love with the now legendary Hamish Macbeth some months before. She had read up on all the cases he had solved. The minute she had heard of the vacancy at Lochdubh, she had promptly applied. In the boot of her car, along with her luggage, was a carton of cookery books. Her mother who lived in Perth had always said that the way to a man's heart was through the kitchen door.

The sun shone down on the melting snow in the road in front of her. Mountains soared up to a newly washed blue sky. Perth, where Josie had been brought up, was just south of the highland line, and family visits had always been to the south – to Glasgow or Edinburgh. She found the whole idea of the Highlands romantic.

As her little Toyota cruised down into

Lochdubh, she gave a gasp of delight. White-washed eighteenth-century cottages fronted the still waters of the sea loch. The pine forest on the other side of the loch was reflected in its waters. Melting snow sparkled in the sunlight.

The police station had an old-fashioned blue lamp hanging outside. Josie drew up and parked her car. She could already imagine herself cooking delicious meals for Hamish while he smiled at her fondly and said, 'Whatever did I do without you?'

The front gate was difficult to open. She finally managed and went up the short path to the door and knocked loudly.

A muffled voice from the other side of the door reached her ears. 'Go round to the side door.'

Back out and round the side of the police station went Josie. Hamish Macbeth was standing by the open kitchen door looking down at her quizzically.

'I'm Josie McSween,' said Josie. 'I'll just get my things.'

'You can't move in here,' said Hamish. 'The villagers won't have it. You're to stay with Mrs Wellington, the minister's wife.'

'But –'

'There are no buts about it. The ladies of the village won't thole a lassie living with me at the police station. I'll get my coat and walk ye up there. When you see where it is, you can come back for your car. Wait there, McSween, I'll get my coat.'

McSween! In all her dreams he had called her Josie. Hamish emerged shortly and began to walk off with long strides in the direction of the manse while Josie scurried behind him.

'Don't I get a choice of where I want to live?' she panted.

'You're a policewoman,' said Hamish over his shoulder. 'You just go where you're put.'

The manse was situated behind the church. It was a Georgian building. Georgian architecture usually conjures a vision of elegance, but Scottish Georgian can be pretty functional and bleak. It was a square three-storey sandstone building, unornamented, and with several windows bricked up dating from the days of the window tax.

Hamish led the way round to the kitchen door where Mrs Wellington was already waiting, the highland bush telegraph having noticed and relayed every moment of Josie's arrival.

Josie's heart sank even lower. Mrs Wellington was a vast tweedy woman with a booming voice.

'Where are your things?' she asked.

'I left them in my car at the police station,' said Josie.

'Shouldn't you be in uniform?'

'It's my day off.'

'Off you go, Mr Macbeth,' said Mrs Wellington. 'I'll just show Miss McSween her room and give her the rules of the house and then she can bring her luggage.'

Josie followed Mrs Wellington into the manse kitchen. It was vast, dating from the days when ministers had servants and large families. It was stone-flagged, and the double sinks by the window were deep and made of stone with old-fashioned brass taps. A long dresser lining one wall contained blue and white plates. The newest item was a scarlet fuel-burning Raeburn stove. High up in the ceiling by a wooden pulley burned a dim single lightbulb. On the pulley hung a row of Mrs Wellington's knickers: large, cotton, and fastened at the knee with elastic. Where on earth did one get knickers like that these days, wondered Josie. People didn't often talk about knickers any more, preferring the American *panties*. But *panties* suggested something naughty and feminine. In one corner stood a large fridge and, wonder of wonders in this antique place, a dishwasher.

'Come along,' ordered Mrs Wellington. 'The washing machine is in the laundry room over there to your left. Washing is on Thursdays.'

Josie followed her out of the kitchen, which led into a dark hall where a few dim, badly painted portraits of previous ministers stared down at her. There was a hallstand of the kind that looked like an altar and a Benares brass bowl full of dusty pampas grass.

The staircase was of stone, the steps worn smooth and polished by the long years of feet pounding up and down. At the first landing, Mrs Wellington led the way along a corridor painted acid green on the top half, the bottom half being made of strips of brown-painted wood.

The wind had risen, and it moaned about the old manse like a banshee. Mrs Wellington pushed open a door at the end. 'This is where you'll stay. The arrangement is for bed and breakfast. Any other meals you want you will cook yourself, but not between five and six which is when I prepare tea for Mr Wellington.'

To Josie's relief the room was light and cheerful. The window looked out over the roofs of the waterfront houses to the loch. There was a large double bed with a splendid patchwork quilt covering it. A peat fire was burning in the hearth.

'We are fortunate to have a large supply of the peat so you can burn as much as you like,' said Mrs Wellington. 'Now, once you are settled in, you will have your tea with us, seeing as it is your first day, and in the evening I will take you to a meeting of the Mothers'

Union in the church hall to introduce you to the other ladies of Lochdubh.'

'But Hamish –' began Josie weakly.

'I have told him of the arrangements and he has agreed. You are to report to the police station tomorrow morning at nine o'clock. When you drive up, you can leave your car outside the front door for easy access, but after that, use the kitchen door. Here are the keys. The only one you need to use is the kitchen door key.'

The key was a large one, no doubt dating from when the manse had been built.

Josie thanked her and scurried off down the stairs. The mercurial weather had changed and a squall of sleet struck her in the face. She had been to the hairdresser only that morning. On her way back to the police station, the malicious wind whipped her hair this way and that, and gusts of icy sleet punched her in the face.

She knocked at the police station door but there was no answer. Josie got into her car and drove up to the manse.

She struggled up the stairs with two large suitcases. The manse was silent except for the moan of the wind.

In her room, there was a huge Victorian wardrobe straight out of Narnia. She hung away her clothes. Josie wanted a long hot bath. She walked along the corridor, nervously pushing open door after door until she found a large bathroom at the end. There was a claw-footed bath with a gas heater over it. The heater looked ancient but the meter down on the floor looked new. She crouched down and read the instructions. 'Place a one-pound coin in the meter and turn the dial to the left and then to the right. Light the geyser and stand back.' On a shelf beside the bath was a box of long matches.

Josie returned to her room and changed into her dressing gown, found a pound coin, and went back to the bathroom. She put the coin in the meter and twisted the dial, then turned on the water. There was a hiss of gas. She fumbled anxiously with the box of matches, lit one, and poked it into the meter. There was a terrifying bang as the gas lit but the stream of water became hot.

The bath was old and deep and took about half an hour to fill. At last, she sank into it and wondered what she was going to do about Hamish Macbeth. Perhaps the village women at the church hall could fill her in with some details.

Hamish Macbeth crowed over the phone to Jimmy Anderson. 'I'm telling you, I give that lassie two days at the most. By the time Mrs

Wellington's finished with her, she'll be crying for a transfer back to Strathbane.'

Josie decided that evening to dress in her uniform to give herself a bit of gravitas. She still felt hungry. She was used to dinner in the evening, not the high tea served in homes in Lochdubh. She had eaten a small piece of fish with a portion of canned peas and one boiled potato followed by two very hard tea cakes.

To her relief, there were cakes, sandwiches, and tea on offer at the village hall. Mrs Wellington introduced her all round. Josie wondered if she would ever remember all the names. One woman with a gentle face and wispy hair stood out – Angela Brodie, the doctor's wife – and two fussy old twins called Nessie and Jessie Currie.

Over the teacups, Nessie and Jessie warned her that Hamish Macbeth was a philanderer and to stick to her job but Angela rescued her and said, mildly, that usually the trouble started because of women pursuing Hamish, not the other way around.

Josie tossed her newly washed hair. She had carried her cap under her arm so as not to spoil the hairstyle. She was angry with Hamish for billeting her at the manse and spoiling her dreams. 'I can't see what anyone would see in the man,' said Josie. 'He's just a long drip with that funny-looking red hair.'

'Hamish Macbeth is a friend of mine and, may I add, your boss,' said Angela and walked away.

Josie bit her lip in vexation. This was no way to go about making friends. She hurried after Angela. 'Look here, that was a stupid thing to say. The fact is I don't really want to stay at the manse. It's a bit like being in boarding school. I'm angry with Hamish for not finding me somewhere a bit more congenial.'

'Oh, you'll get used to it,' said Angela. 'Hamish covers a huge beat. You'll be out all day.'

The next morning, Hamish presented Josie with ordnance survey maps and a long list of names and addresses. 'These are elderly people who live alone in the remoter areas,' he said. 'It's part of our duties to periodically check up on them. You won't be able to do it all in one day or maybe two. We only have the one vehicle so you'll need to use your own. Give me any petrol receipts and I'll get the money back for you.'

Josie longed to ask him what he was going to do, but had decided her best plan was to be quiet and willing until he cracked. And she was sure he would crack and realize what wife potential he had under his highland nose.

She gave him her mobile phone number and set out, deciding to try some of the faraway addresses first. Josie drove along, up and down the single-track roads of Sutherland, lost in a happy dream.

The hard fact was that she should never have joined the police force. But a television drama, *The Bill*, had fired her imagination. By fantasizing herself into the character of a strong and competent policewoman, she had passed through her training fairly easily. Her sunny nature made her popular. She had not been in Strathbane long enough for any really nasty cases to wake her up to the realities of her job. She baked cakes for the other constables, asked about their wives and families, and generally made herself well liked. She was given easy assignments.

Then one day after she had been in Strathbane only a few weeks, Hamish Macbeth strolled into police headquarters. Josie took one look at his tall figure, flaming red hair, and hazel eyes and decided she was in love. And since she was already in love with some sort of Brigadoon idea of the Highlands, she felt that Hamish Macbeth was a romantic figure.

Hamish Macbeth began to receive telephone calls from people in the outlying crofts praising Josie McSween. She was described as 'a ray of sunshine', 'a ministering angel', and 'a fine wee lassie'.

As there was no crime on his beat and Josie was covering what would normally be his duties, Hamish found himself at liberty to mooch around the village and go fishing.

During the late afternoon, with his dog and cat at his heels, he strolled around to see his friend Angela Brodie, the doctor's wife. Angela was a writer, always in the throes of trying to produce another book. She typed on her laptop at the kitchen table where the cats prowled amongst the lunch debris which Angela had forgotten to clear away.

'You'll need to lock your beasts in the living room,' said Angela. 'Sonsie frightens my cats.'

'I'll let them run outside,' said Hamish, shooing his pets out the door. 'They'll be fine. How's it going?'

'Not very well. I had a visit from a French writer. One of my books has been translated into French. She spoke excellent English, which is just as well because I have only school French. I think I upset her.'

'How?'

'Pour yourself some coffee. It's like this. She talked about the glories of being a writer. She said it was a spiritual experience. She said this must be a marvellous place for inspiration. Well, you know, writers who wait for inspiration get mental block. One just slogs on. I said so. She got very high and mighty and said I could not be a real writer. She said, "Pouf!"'

'Meaning?'

'It's that sort of sound that escapes the French mouth when they make a *moue* of contempt.'

'I haven't seen a tourist here in ages,' said Hamish, sitting down opposite her. 'The Americans can't afford to come this far and the French are tied up in the credit crunch.'

'By the way she was dressed, she had private means. I bet she published her books herself,' said Angela. 'How's your new copper?'

'Rapidly on her way to becoming the saint o' Sutherland. I sent her off to check on the isolated folks and they've been phoning me up to say how marvellous she is. Every time I go back to the police station, there's another one ringing in wi' an accolade.'

Angela leaned back in her chair. 'What's she after?'

'What do you mean?'

'A pretty little girl like that doesn't want to be buried up here in the wilds unless she has some sort of agenda.'

'I don't think she has. I think she was simply told to go. Jimmy said she had volunteered but I find that hard to believe.'

'Had she met you before?'

'No. First I saw of her was when she landed on my doorstep.' Hamish had not even noticed Josie that time when she had first seen him at police headquarters. 'Anyway, as long as she keeps out o' ma hair, we'll get along just fine.'

By the time the days dragged on until the end of June, Josie was bored. There was no way of getting to him. She could not tempt him with beautiful meals because Mrs Wellington had decided not to let her use the kitchen, saying if she wanted an evening meal she would cook it and bill headquarters for the extra expense, and when, one evening, Josie plucked up courage and suggested to Hamish that she would cook a meal for them both, he had said, 'Don't worry, McSween. I'm going out.'

It wasn't that Hamish did not like his constable, it was simply that he valued his privacy and thought that letting any woman work in his kitchen was a bad idea. Look what had happened when he had been briefly engaged to Priscilla Halburton-Smythe. Without consulting him, she'd had his beloved stove removed and a nasty electric cooker put in instead. No, you just couldn't let a woman in the kitchen.

Josie had three weeks' holiday owing. She decided to spend it with her mother in Perth. Her mother always knew what to do.

* * *

Josie was an only child, and Mrs Flora McSween had brought her daughter up on a diet of romantic fiction. Just before she arrived, Flora had been absorbed in the latest issue of *The People's Friend. The People's Friend* magazine had grown and prospered by sticking to the same formula of publishing romantic stories. While other women's magazines had stopped publishing fiction and preferred hard-hitting articles such as 'I Had My Father's Baby' and other exposés, *People's Friend* went its own sweet way, adding more and more stories as its circulation rose. It also contained articles on Scotland, recipes, poetry, knitting patterns, notes from a minister, and advice from an agony aunt.

The arrival of her copy was the highlight of Flora's week. When her daughter burst in the door, saying, 'It's no good, Ma. He's barely aware of my existence,' Flora knew exactly who she was talking about, her daughter having shared her romantic dreams about Hamish over the phone.

'Now, pet,' said Flora, 'sit down and take your coat off and I'll make us a nice cup of tea. Faint heart never won a gentleman. Maybe you've been trying too hard.'

'He calls me McSween, he sends me off hundreds of miles to check on boring old people and make sure they're all right. I'm so tired of smiling and drinking tea and eating scones, I could scream.'

'You know what would bring you together? A nice juicy crime.'

'So what if there isn't one in that backwater? What do I do? Murder someone?'

FREEPOST RLUL-SJGC-SGKJ, Cash Sales Direct Mail Dept., The Book Service, Colchester Road, Frating, Colchester, CO7 7DW. Tel: +44 (0) 1206 255 800.
Fax: +44 (0) 1206 255 930. Email: sales@tbs-ltd.co.uk

UK customers: please allow £1.00 p&p for the first book, plus 50p for the second, and an additional 30p for each book thereafter, up to a maximum charge of £3.00. Overseas customers (incl. Ireland): please allow £2.00 p&p for the first book, plus £1.00 for the second, plus 50p for each additional book.

NAME (block letters): ______________________________

ADDRESS: ______________________________

____

______________________ POSTCODE: ______________

I enclose a cheque/PO (payable to 'TBS Direct') for the amount

of £__________________

I wish to pay by Switch/Credit Card

Card number: ______________________________

Expiry date: __________ Switch issue number: __________